Pra~~ise for~~

Dialogues with the Wise Woman

Dialogues with the Wise Woman by author Richard Todd Devens is a no-holds-barred quest for certitude and a psychological and philosophic treatise that tackles many substantial matters such as the nature of wickedness, the determination of good and bad, the rationale of vengeance, and the ethical handling of crime and epidemics, among others...This is a text that showcases a form of self-torture human beings often subject themselves to, whenever hurtful memories from the past come knocking. As Mildred reveals, such occurrences keep happening because people tend to feel a sense of shame and pain, which they easily interpret as a sign of failure and weakness. As the book delves deeper, readers will come across supporting tales from various persons, who equally let toxic poison into their brains, giving way to self-imposed pain, low self-esteem, and venomous internal criticism...Dazzling with hearty discussions, wise excerpts, sensible arguments, and warm associations, *Dialogues with the Wise Woman* by Richard Todd Devens is a text you will want to acquire for its insightful sense which stands crucial in day-to-day undertakings. I highly recommend the read to anyone who desires raw, brutally honest, and practical orientation into defeating life's plights and distresses.

—*Hollywood Book Reviews (starred review)*

While the book may not have a traditional narrative structure, it captivates readers through the sessions between George and Mildred, where they reflect on past experiences and valuable lessons learned...readers can glean valuable insights from her sessions with George, almost as if they were personally engaging with a therapist...George's pain and vulnerability after falling victim to a scam will resonate deeply with readers who have experienced similar situations...*Dialogues with the Wise Woman* by Richard Todd Devens is an excellent choice for readers seeking fiction that addresses societal issues and provokes contemplation.

—*Portland Book Review*

...fascinating conversations involving smart thinkers and knowledge seekers... The story's several engaging dialogues present a wealth of insightful concepts and conundrums that will lead the reader to reflect deeply and gain new understanding. Several concerns are addressed in a way that casts fresh light on certain topics. Furthermore, the book is filled with quotable lines and thought-provoking queries that plant seeds of knowledge and empower readers to draw their own conclusions - or at least, have an open mind - about the topics covered. I came upon a number of wise words that seemed to illuminate parts of my brain that had been dormant...Devens' words are typically beautiful, intellectually fascinating, and vividly descriptive. The discussions provide an opportunity to learn how to look at things from multiple perspectives and to investigate contradictions, inconsistencies, and exceptions in various philosophies...will appeal to readers who enjoy philosophical fiction that ignites intelligent thoughts. It contains various conundrums and ironies that will keep the reader entertained long after the book is done...*Dialogues with the Wise Woman* is an amazing book that incorporates principles that I feel everyone should have, such as discussing challenging beliefs, listening, and asking uncomfortable questions. It teaches readers to investigate things and embrace an all-encompassing perspective that brings about rising above restrictive beliefs. It's not your typical narrative, but it offers a lot of value in a compact package.

—*Manhattan Book Review*

Dialogues with the Wise Woman are conversations between caring adults, fructified by generous helpings of compassion and insight, transcribed by the author from his imagination...The resulting conversations read like recovered treasure - - like Dead Sea Scrolls freighted with pearls of insight and contemporary relevance. Devens' book stands on the shoulders of psycho-conversational giants like Irvin Yalom, Oliver Sacks and Abraham Verghese before him...The episodes and choice of subjects are, frankly, delightful...Imagination, vivacity, and a fine brush stroke are very much evident here. Devens' book, and we hope there will be more from him of this genre, excels not only at individual and personal portraiture, but he is able to capture the sweep and majesty of an authentic white-knuckled chokehold on the Real.

—*Pacific Book Review*

Matters of the mind and heart, and right and wrong, are contemplated deeply... Richard Todd Devens certainly gives readers a lot to think about in his heady *Dialogues with the Wise Woman*. It forces readers to put themselves in many "what if" situations and contemplate what they would do. And it's fascinating to listen to the dialogue and points of view - on the therapist's couch and in a crowded auditorium.

—*BookTrib*

With heavy themes of self-awareness, self-assurance, and self-love, *Dialogues with the Wise Woman* is a heart-warming journey into self-discovery and the kindness of those around us...Devens artfully crafts the characters and story to be both lifelike and to demonstrate the truth...This is a unique, thought-provoking portrait of a character, a therapy relationship, and what it means to be human.

—*BookLife Reviews*

Dialogues with the Wise Woman, by Richard Todd Devens, is an enlightening exploration of human psychology and the quest for meaning. Devens weaves a captivating narrative through engaging dialogues and profound insights, guiding readers on a thought-provoking journey alongside the troubled character, George Sistern...In his pursuit of healing, George seeks solace in the company of psychotherapist, Mildred Markowitz. Their dialogues touch on issues of self-esteem, violent crime, and the philosophy of self-improvement, offering readers a profound reflection on their own lives and choices...What stands out in this book is Devens' ability to weave a story around the myriad of issues raised. Devens' narrative brims with wisdom, inviting readers to explore the complexities of life, morals, and ethics... its unique storytelling style infuses the journey with a distinctive flavor...*Dialogues with the Wise Woman* delivers refreshing and insightful perspectives that resonate with a variety of readers. For those who might find philosophy and therapy daunting, this book illuminates pathways toward inner conviction and liberation. Richard Todd Devens has crafted a compelling narrative that encourages introspection and self-discovery, making it a valuable addition to the genre of psychological and philosophical literature.

—*Literary Titan*

DIALOGUES
WITH THE
WISE WOMAN

DIALOGUES
WITH THE
WISE WOMAN

RICHARD TODD DEVENS

gatekeeper press™
Tampa, Florida

This book is a work of fiction. The names, characters and events in this book are the products of the author's imagination or are used fictitiously. Any similarity to real persons living or dead is coincidental and not intended by the author.

The views and opinions expressed in this book are solely those of the author and do not reflect the views or opinions of Gatekeeper Press. Gatekeeper Press is not to be held responsible for and expressly disclaims responsibility for the content herein.

Dialogues with the Wise Woman

Published by Gatekeeper Press
7853 Gunn Hwy., Suite 209
Tampa, FL 33626
www.GatekeeperPress.com

Library of Congress Control Number: 2022952334

ISBN (paperback): 9781662933219
eISBN: 9781662933226

To Joseph Devens

PREFACE

Sometime after the publication of *Rational Polemics*, I had the idea of writing a novel, so I could illustrate my philosophy through the dialogue of fictional characters. After completing it, I sent it to an editor. After reading it, she informed me that I had a steep learning curve ahead of me if I aspired to write fiction that would work. She wrote that writing fiction is much harder than writing nonfiction, and that my "novel" was really not a novel at all, but basically several hundred pages of dialogue. One of the rules of fiction writing, she explained, is "show me, don't tell me." Her critique, as well as all her comments, were astute and absolutely correct.

I respect the enormous skill required to write fiction at the highest level. It incorporates storytelling, theme, plot, subplot, conflict, resolution, characterization, pace, etc. Although *Dialogues with the Wise Woman* (a totally different manuscript than the one I had previously written) would most accurately be classified as fiction, I did not want to confine myself to its constraints. I love dialogue, and in some instances, I prefer to use it rather than just delivering cold, hard information or my point of view. I can present opposing points of view, play devil's advocate, and then allow the reader to make up his or her own mind as to which viewpoint is "right."

I can create a debate by having one of the parties argue against or have a different take on an issue than another person. That way, a reader's opinion would probably have already been taken into account. They would not even necessarily know which viewpoint I held, and there would often be no clear-cut indication as to who had "won" the debate. Sometimes, there might not even *be* a "right" answer to a particular dilemma or problem. The reader could take into account the opposing views, and would be free to make up his or her *own* mind.

Two particular films come to mind when I think of the relationship between a patient and his therapist: *Ordinary People* and *Good Will Hunting*. The dialogue during the therapy sessions is what I found most memorable.

Often, when someone is in acute emotional pain and is experiencing severe anguish, there is no *time* to explore someone's upbringing and context. Additionally, the solutions to some of the torture that we inflict upon ourselves can be mitigated by an analysis of the situation...and by not only learning a different way to think about the situation, but learning how to avoid having the same situation ever come up again. Very often, our *thoughts* about a situation determine its severity. Two people can experience the same situation. One considers it a "disaster"; the other uses it as a learning experience. This brings to mind a quote that Dr. Wayne Dyer often cited: "If you change the way you look at things, the things you look at change."

Almost everyone has experienced the little annoyances that are a part of life: You're rushing out the door and your shoelace breaks, or a button pops off your pants or shirt. Very often, people allow this trivia to get blown entirely out of proportion. Then there are worse things that happen: You get an unjust traffic ticket; you're involved in a fender bender; a motorist hurls obscenities at you when you've done nothing wrong. Again, different people will react differently to the same situation. But a mature and rational person, while not pretending to enjoy the situation, is able to put it in perspective, and realizes that these things are not as bad as having cancer, being raped, having a loved one killed, or having your home destroyed in a hurricane.

I have always imagined a *wise woman*. Someone would be in severe emotional pain and would figuratively be sinking in quicksand. He or she saw no way out of the abyss. Just getting through everyday life, and performing the chores we all do, represented an enormous challenge. But the wise woman would be there to provide understanding, as well as profound insight and wisdom. She would save people's lives and uplift their spirit; she would give them a reason to go on.

She doesn't discount nor trivialize a person's upbringing and past experiences as the genesis of one's woes. But at the same time, she realizes that when one is in pain, the bleeding must be stopped, just as when one is physically bleeding because of an injury. An exhaustive exploration of one's infancy and adolescence might hold clues as to the "why," but the wise woman would be more concerned with the "how": what we can do in the present to address the demons that are causing immobilization, and what we can learn and *do* to prevent future suffering.

CHAPTER ONE

George Sistern was a forty-six-year-old pianist. Because of the nature of his work, he could never count on a steady stream of income. There could be long gaps between gigs, and students would come and go. He did odd jobs to pay his bills.

Not having a woman in his life drove him to do something that eventually led to him being scammed by a Las Vegas con artist. Although it wasn't a huge amount of money, the fact that he ignored all the red flags that had been staring him in the face, and ignored the words of a woman who had given him the wisest advice anyone could've possibly given him on the subject, drove him to a deep depression. No matter how hard he tried, he couldn't let go of the rage and hatred he had for the scammer, and couldn't live with his stupidity for allowing it to happen.

On two separate occasions, acquaintances asked him what was wrong. When the latest person asked, a woman named Francine, George said he appreciated her concern, but it wasn't something he wanted to discuss. Francine said she didn't mean to pry, but it was obvious something was wrong, and she didn't like seeing him this way. "I think you should see Mildred," she said, jotting her name and number down on a piece of paper.

This wasn't the first time George had heard her name. He asked Francine who she was, and she told him that Mildred was a therapist of the rarest kind—a brilliant, wonderful, insightful woman who was kind, caring, loving, and compassionate. She was a true motherly figure, but at the same time didn't bullshit people and tell them what they wanted to hear. She believed in cutting to the chase, attacking and solving problems the same way a dentist extracts a rotten tooth. The patient was ultimately responsible for doing the work, but Mildred would provide the insight and wisdom that would ignite in her patients the courage to fight for their lives.

Mildred Markowitz was sixty-seven years old. Overweight, matronly, and not conventionally attractive, she was down-to-earth, unassuming, warm, and friendly. She was the kind of woman whom you might expect to be running a grocery store in a wooded rural town, miles from civilization. Or perhaps she might've been a painter or a woman who hooked rugs. She was happily married to Jim, a math professor and Fields Medal winner who was something of a legend in his field. He was like the male equivalent of Mildred, except that he was tall, thin, and handsome. They lived in a building on Mercer Street in Manhattan's SoHo district, but also owned a summer cottage on three acres in Vermont.

Although she rarely talked about it unless she was asked, Mildred held a PhD in psychology and philosophy. Ever since she was young, she'd had an avid fascination for the human mind. She was concerned with what motivated people and what factors contributed to neuroses. She believed that, barring chemical imbalances, there were almost always practical solutions to problems.

In her books and articles, she argued that psychology and philosophy shouldn't be divorced from one another. A highly skilled psychologist can explore a patient's past in order to come up with reasons or patterns which explain present-day thought, behaviors, and perceptions. On rare occasions, a patient receives life-altering insight which often acts as a catharsis, like vomiting out poisonous toxins from the past. The patient is set free of an enormous burden they've been carrying around with them.

Unfortunately, when dealing with something as complex as the human mind, there's so much that is still nebulous. That's why psychiatry and psychology are often called inexact sciences. We know, for example, that certain areas of the brain are responsible for various emotions, such as depression, and we know that this has to do with serotonin levels. Antidepressants *have* helped the seriously depressed when the depression was primarily caused by a physical imbalance in the brain. But very often, a psychiatrist has to "play peekaboo" (as one doctor calls it) with the meds in order to determine what's most beneficial; it's hit or miss.

They *have* helped many people, and some people have said that they wouldn't have been able to live and function without them. And if meds made the difference between a person committing suicide or not, then the advantages certainly outweighed the disadvantages in those cases. But there are also instances of meds exacerbating a preexisting condition, and causing dependency and addiction. And what about the situations in which a person is seriously depressed or has serious problems because of reasons *unrelated* to chemical imbalances in the brain?

People experience grief and serious depression because of traumas, and because of experiences that have left them feeling worthless and hopeless. Often, by uncovering the genesis of these feelings, and their implications, a skilled therapist can guide a person out of the "tunnel," or help them to escape the bars of their self-inflicted prison. But because the world of emotions and feelings are so fraught with nebulousness, and because the understanding of the workings and complexities of the human brain are still in their infancy—as is our knowledge of the infinity of the universe—it's very hard to weed out the unskilled and the charlatans unless they're caught in egregious instances of unethical behavior.

Mildred believed that philosophy offers the counterbalance of reason and logic. The utilization of both psychology *and* philosophy can help guide a person to make more sensible decisions. She also studied chi (the focusing of internal energy that many martial artists and Asian masters have utilized), because of its relation to psychology and the human brain.

When asked in an interview for an example of how utilizing philosophy could help someone make a better decision than by merely employing psychology, she began by asking a question of the interviewer: "Let's look at gambling. Have you ever been to Vegas?"

"Yes, but I don't know a thing about gambling."

"Neither do I. But I do know something about the human emotion greed, and its motivation for getting something for nothing. Let's suppose you went to Vegas to play blackjack, and you're not one of those MIT whiz kids who study the game, practice, have a system, and therefore stack the odds in their favor. What do you think the chances would be that you'd go home with less money than when you started?"

"About 99 percent."

"Precisely. Now, if it's understood by the average person that it's highly unlikely they'll win, that a day at a casino is purely recreational, and that limits should be set beforehand as to the maximum amount they're willing to lose, then there's not much harm in playing. But because once in a while people win, they fantasize that this will be them too. They end up gambling more money than they can afford to lose, and end up throwing good money after bad in an attempt to recoup their losses…which of course, almost never works. Highly educated and intelligent people fall victim to this, because they've allowed their emotions to overrule their intellect.

"A similar situation occurs in relation to sex. A married man, or one in a relationship, meets a drop-dead gorgeous woman at a convention and has the opportunity to have sex with her. He knows all the bad things that can happen if he succumbs to this one isolated encounter, but he's willing to gamble that he'll get away with it. In other words, he wants to have his cake and eat it too. Here's another case of emotions overruling the intellect, and just like with gambling in Vegas, highly educated and intelligent men have repeatedly been unable to resist the temptation.

"The examples are endless. A morbidly obese person decides to 'live for the moment' and will eat bacon double cheeseburgers and French fries on a daily basis. People addicted to drugs, cigarettes, or alcohol will continue to partake. Sometimes, in a traffic altercation, the perpetrator spews obscenities at the innocent driver, and the latter gets so enraged that he physically attacks the other person. Let's say the perpetrator ends up being killed. It now doesn't matter whose fault it was initially. An intelligent and productive family man has now thrown his life away, because he was goaded into seeking revenge."

Mildred charged a large fee for her services, and had her share of high-powered and celebrity patients. But she didn't turn away people who were unable to pay her fee. This was done less out of benevolence than for the simple reason that she didn't want money to be the arbiter as to who could benefit from her services. It was also done for selfish purposes: Each case she was presented with afforded her the opportunity to hone and to test her skills. In those cases she either accepted payment of whatever people could afford, or would barter with the patient for products or services she needed. In any case, a patient was not to feel guilty for receiving "charity." This would cause a distraction that might undermine the therapy.

She was asked about a possible scenario of someone legitimately being able to afford her services, but feigning poverty. Her answer was that anything less than complete honesty on the part of the patient would similarly undermine the effectiveness of the therapy.

She was known for making herself available on short notice, because she realized that not all emergencies were medical. A person who was in a car accident and was hemorrhaging, or a person who had a heart attack or stroke, obviously needed immediate medical attention, so a person in acute mental agony at three o'clock in the morning shouldn't have to wait until "business hours" on weekdays, much less several weeks, because it's more convenient for the doctor.

She was also known for making her patients totally comfortable during their sessions. If a male patient felt compelled to use profanity, he wasn't to hold back just because he thought it might be improper to speak this way in front of a woman; if a man or a woman had to cry, he or she should cry. Even if someone had to fart, by holding it in their full attention couldn't be given to the therapy. A person didn't have to be embarrassed or self-conscious for being human.

Mildred *did* have rules, however. Sessions were not to be interrupted except in an emergency. Cell phones were to be turned off. She, in turn, would not take any calls during sessions. Another thing she was known for was not scheduling patients back-to-back. She didn't believe in the artificial constraints of time limits. If she were in the middle of a vitally important discourse with a patient, and a potential cathartic moment were imminent, to break the mood because "time was up" would be no different than answering a blaring cell phone. By doing so, it'd be making the needs of the caller (who, let's face it, would often be a telemarketer) more important than her patient.

George hesitated for several days. He knew that whatever it was, he wouldn't remotely be able to afford her fee. But money aside, he was also apprehensive about baring all his emotional baggage only to find out she was no good. This had happened many times in the past. But finally, he forced himself to dial the number Francine had given him. He was glad when the call went to voicemail. Maybe she'd be like most people and not return the call. Then he could at least tell Francine that he'd tried. But about two hours later his phone rang, and a friendly voice asked if this was George Sistern. "Speaking," he said.

"This is Mildred Markowitz. How do you do?"

"Hello, Doctor Markowitz."

"Please, call me Mildred."

"Hello, Mildred. I'm sorry to bother you, but Francine gave me your name. She said I should call you."

"Please don't think that you're bothering me. You sound very distressed. I have appointments until eight o'clock this evening, and we could plan to meet at eight thirty. But if this is urgent, I could probably switch some appointments around."

"Oh, no. Don't do that. It's not an emergency. Only, can I ask what your fee is?"

"I charge 300 dollars per session for those who can afford it."

"Oh, I'm so sorry, but there's no way I could afford that."

"Please, don't worry about that. Why don't you come in anyway? I'm sure we can work something out. You sound like you need someone to talk to."

"I do. But I'd feel guilty accepting charity."

"Who said it'd be charity? Look, just come in and we can discuss it in more detail here."

At 8:30 p.m., George rang the bell at the Mercer Street address Mildred had given him. It was on a deserted industrial street in SoHo. Most of the buildings looked like loading docks, not places where people lived. A tall and friendly man opened the door. "George?"

"Yes."

"Hi. Nice to meet you. I'm Jim Markowitz." He extended his hand for a warm handshake. "Please come in."

George followed Jim down a corridor. The interior belied the exterior. It was spacious and rustic with hardwood floors, and immaculately neat. The living room had bookcases built into the walls, which were adorned with hundreds of books. Jim motioned to a comfortable sofa. "Please, make yourself at home. Mildred will be down in a moment."

About thirty seconds later, Mildred appeared. "George? Hi. Mildred. A pleasure to meet you." Her handshake was as warm as Jim's. "I'm preparing some herbal tea. Would you like some?"

"Sure. Mildred, about your fee…"

Mildred waved him off. "What kind of work do you do, George?

"I'm a pianist."

"How wonderful. Jim and I are rabid music lovers. We both took piano lessons when we were young, but as so often happens, life got in the way. Whenever we hear a great one, we both say we'd sell ourselves to the devil to play like that. Come here. I want to show you something." She led George to what looked like a large ballroom. At the end of it, in the center, was a magnificent Steinway concert grand. "We often hold cocktail parties and hire pianists for them. But we also have actual concerts here as well. We have friends who are concert pianists, and they come here to try out their programs. We also have musicians playing chamber music all the time. Perhaps we could use your services as your form of payment for the therapy. Would that be something you might be interested in?"

"Absolutely," said George.

"Great. We'll put the issue of money on hold for now. Let's get to work." She led George further down the corridor to her office, handed him a glass of herbal tea, and they both sat down facing one another. "You're distressed and in pain."

"Yes." George was already impressed. "I did something very stupid."

"Welcome to the club."

"No. This wasn't just stupid."

"It was so stupid that you're beating yourself up over it, and having trouble living with yourself. Like I said, welcome to the club. Welcome to the human race."

"Drunk drivers are human, too."

"Yes, but they hurt innocent people. I don't think you've hurt any innocent people other than yourself. But do you know what? It's even worse to hurt yourself than to hurt another person. Tell me what happened."

"Alright. I'm forty-six years old, don't have a girlfriend, and have never been in a relationship." He looked at Mildred and waited for the inevitable reaction of surprise or question for the reason why. She didn't react, however. "Anyway, I post personal ads on Craigslist all the time, in different cities. They're headlined 'Gamble for Me.' In it, I write that I love going to Vegas, but don't know a thing about gambling. 'If you're a drop-dead gorgeous woman who's a highly skilled gambler,' I write, 'I'll let you gamble with my money. If you win, you keep 50 percent of the winnings.' Not bad for not risking a penny of your own money, in my opinion. 'But if you lose, you have to go out with me to dinner and a show.' In my ad, I say that this isn't a clever ploy to date women. I say I'm in top condition, and don't have trouble finding women. The 'going out on a date' thing is just my safety net, to make sure the women are taking it as seriously as I am."

"Sounds pretty reasonable to me. Why should you be the only one putting up stakes, so to speak?"

"Exactly. I explain that no matter how attractive the woman might be, winning money was my primary objective. Anyway, these meetups are notoriously hit-and-miss, and some just end up being not worth my time at all. To give you one example, several years ago a woman responded to one of these ads, and told me she was a champion Bingo player who regularly won a lot of money, and was very particular where she played. She assured me she'd show me how it felt to win in Vegas. She even called me before I was scheduled to fly in to try to get me to come to town immediately, because she was 'on a roll.'"

"I'm sure you know that Bingo is a game of total chance and luck."

"Ever so well."

"Did you end up being attracted to her?"

"Not at all. She was the kind of woman you'd pay *not* to date. When I arrived in town, she urged me to rush to the Palace Station right away, so I'd be in time for the next game. So I took a cab downtown rather than wait for the free shuttle. When I got there, she said I should put up my whole stake, 700 dollars, for two games. When I asked why we couldn't just play one game so I'd have some money left over for the remaining days, she said, 'Don't worry. We'll win, and we'll use the money for the next couple of days.'"

"So you staked the entire 700 dollars and lost it all."

"How'd you guess? So anyway, I posted a similar ad about three years ago, and received a response from a woman who called herself Victoria, and referred to herself as 'The Poker Queen.'"

"She *called* herself Victoria?"

"That's right. Her real name is Celestial Rimas."

"Did you ask why she called herself Victoria?"

"Yeah. She said it was her 'poker name.'"

"I see."

"She said she was a great poker player who'd been playing for many years, had won tournaments, and had beaten top players. She wanted this to be a fruitful and productive business partnership."

"So what was going through your mind?"

"Something bothered me about her voice and her manner; I couldn't put my finger on it. But she *did* seem like she was probably a highly skilled player."

"And that was more important to you than her being attractive."

"All things being equal, yes. I'd rather have an obese wrinkled-up ninety-year-old woman who was highly skilled and won money for me, than a gorgeous bimbo who lost it all."

"Even if it meant that losing your money would require her to spend an intimate evening with you?"

"That's right. Because even if she *did* lose, who's to say she'd keep her part of the bargain?"

"Precisely. So, you arranged to fly to Vegas to meet the Poker Queen."

"Yes, and agreed to stake her 1,000 dollars that weekend. But even after I'd already booked the flight, she asked if I could send her 200 dollars immediately, because she wanted to compete in a big tournament coming up before I got there. Her most oft-repeated refrain, both before and after we met, was, 'My word is my bond,' and she was always saying her Jewish religion would prevent her from ever doing anything unethical. That was her sole means of proof. She tried getting the money from me a few more times, but eventually backed off.

"Around this time, a guy named Dave answered the same ad that I'd posted on the Las Vegas page of Craigslist. Even though he was a male, the gambling part of the ad is what had caught his attention, and he was curious to know whether posts like these were actually working for me. I told him what I had coming up, and he seemed genuinely concerned. He said this Poker Queen seemed like a scammer. He reminded me that even the best player in the world can lose to a lousy player on a single hand if he has a lousy hand at that particular time. He said that staking 1,000 dollars to play at a high-stakes table, as the Poker Queen had asked for, could result in higher winnings, but could also mean losing it all in a hurry. I asked him if he'd do me a favor and join me when I first met her. He agreed to, and also said he'd ask her a lot of tough technical questions, and that if she couldn't answer them then I shouldn't let her play with my money. He also warned me that he couldn't guarantee he wouldn't lose his temper."

"Okay, so you went to Vegas."

"Yes. I met up with Dave at the Monte Carlo where I was staying, and he told me that everything new he was learning about this 'Poker Queen' was more and more of a red flag, and making him very angry. I called the woman, told her where I was, and eventually she finally showed up."

"And how did she look?"

"Almost as ugly as the Bingo woman. So anyway, Dave is 'qualifying' her and asking her questions about the basics of poker, which the Poker Queen answered to his satisfaction. He was cordial throughout, but at times he raised his voice a little and said, 'You're not answering my question.' At one point, he asked her what she did for a living. She said she was a paralegal, but had recently gotten laid off. Then he asked, 'If you're so great at poker, why do you need to play with other people's money?' Her answer was, 'I'm addicted to slot machines.' Dave said, 'Well, at least she's honest,' and seemed to be satisfied with her answers.

"So I gave her 260 dollars, she gave me her driver's license as collateral, and we agreed to meet in the poker room at the Aria after I went up to my room and got settled in. Dave told me to get there as soon as possible, so I could stay next to her and keep an eye on her at all times, as there'd be almost no way to prevent her from slipping a couple of chips into her pocket. So I rushed over as soon as possible, and was allowed to sit down right beside her."

"And how were you feeling?"

"Scared to death. When I saw that there were almost no chips in front of her, I panicked. She told me not to worry, as she didn't bet all the chips at one time. Anyway, she was actually way ahead when we decided to finally call it a night. She joined me at the booth where people redeem their chips. I took back my 260 dollars, and there was a 315 dollar profit. She asked if we could split just the 300 dollars equally and have the extra 15 dollars be her 'tip,' so I said okay and took my 150-dollar cut.

"Now, to be clear, I don't actually know much about gambling myself, but one of the interesting things about these trips is that it's let me learn a lot of lessons from these women I've interacted with. Never bet more than you can afford to lose; gamble for recreation only and expect to lose as part of that; never let anyone else gamble with your money.' I broke all of these rules on this occasion, and considered myself extremely lucky to have been able to walk away with a 150-dollar profit. Although, it was actually much less once you subtracted all the costs. I had bought meals for Dave and the Poker Queen, given her a 'tip,' and had paid extra for a hotel room with two beds, so she could sleep there between her gambling sessions. And of course, I'd spent over one thousand dollars on my own meals, hotel, and airfare.

"So I decided, especially with Dave's advice, to quit while I was ahead. It would feel far worse to lose after I'd already won than to have never won in the first place. So, after the Poker Queen got some sleep in my hotel room and was ready to resume, I informed her that I didn't want to play anymore."

"And what was her reaction?"

"She said, 'Okay, then there's no reason for me to stay here anymore.' She gathered her things, said, 'Goodbye, George,' and stormed out of the room."

"And how did you feel?"

"Relief. I was glad it was over. Of course, she wanted to win...for *herself*, not for me. But since it was my money, she would've in no way been hurt if she lost. Yet she was angry at me—a poor schnook—for not allowing her to gamble anymore with *my* money. She proved what kind of person she is through her actions.

Earlier, I had asked her why she felt she was so successful at poker. She said that she prayed to the poker god, and had Him on her side. I asked her why He didn't help her when she played the slots, but she didn't answer.

"A couple of hours after she stormed out of the room, my cell phone rang. She was calling to ask if I could spare five dollars so she could take the bus to go home. After she left, she had blown all her money on the slots. Since everything was now over, I thought about saying no, but then I thought that five bucks would be a small price to pay for being able to walk away without losing my money…and I was glad I'd be permanently rid of her."

"But you weren't."

"That's right. About a day later, she started sending me texts, sort of mocking me, telling me it was a shame I'd spent over a thousand dollars to come to Vegas only to back out after having made so little back. She said she could've made six thousand dollars if I had let her keep at it. I don't know whether she meant gross or 6K for each of us, but it didn't really matter to me. To be honest, I did wonder what would've happened if I'd kept letting her play for me."

"What do *you* think would've happened?"

"I think it's in the realm of possibility that she would've hit six thousand, but unlikely. And if she'd lost it all, I'd really be kicking myself for not walking away while I was ahead. Then she undoubtedly would've pressured me to stake more, as her losing would have been explained as a momentary setback that had no bearing on the big picture. I then would have been chasing bad money with good money.

"So anyway, the texts kept coming. One said, 'Dave is an idiot, and I can tell he's not a very good poker player.' She also wrote, 'You said I have nothing to lose, but I'm a winner, and I don't like losing.' And the coup de grâce: 'Do you want me to tell you what Dave really said to you? He said that if I had sex with you, I wouldn't owe you any of my winnings.' Why she thought that sex with such a fat, ugly dog would be even remotely on my mind is beyond me.

"A few days after I got back home to New York, I received a voicemail from the Poker Queen. 'Being a naturally curious person', she said, 'I was wondering what you did during the rest of your stay in Vegas. Did you let Dave play poker for you?'"

"And let me guess, you felt compelled to call back, even though you'd already breathed a sigh of relief that the situation was over and behind you, because you didn't want to be rude." George felt as if Mildred were reading his mind. He stared at her, and Mildred smiled and gently nodded her head. "Did it ever cross your mind to tell her that you actually got really lucky and won a lot of money with Dave?"

"I did think about it later, and asked myself why I didn't just say that. I think it's just my natural motivation to be honest, even though honesty is, of course, not morally required when you're dealing with a dishonest person." They looked at one another again with a mutual knowing smile, which neither had to translate. "But obviously, it would have been better if I simply ignored the message and didn't call back.

"So she launched into a hard sell again about how I should bankroll her gambling. She said I didn't even have to come to Vegas; I could just mail her money, she would play, and then mail me back half the winnings in addition to what I sent her. We could do this every week and have a very profitable partnership. I asked her if she'd verify everything that she did and provide photos and paperwork, and she said yes. I hemmed and hawed about it for a while." He went silent.

Mildred touched George gently on the knee. "So you mailed her money?" She said it more as a statement than a question.

George looked down at the floor and nodded.

"Yes, I mailed her 500 dollars. I continued to ignore all the red flags. She said she lived in Henderson, but gave me a Las Vegas address. She didn't have a bank account, so she had to cash my check at a check-cashing place which charged her a twenty-five dollar fee. Then I didn't hear from her at all, and started to panic. After two days, I couldn't take it anymore, so I called the two numbers I had, and left voicemails. I still didn't hear back, so I emailed her and called her a thief.

"Sometime later, she emailed me back to let me know that it was Yom Kippur and she had just finished a period of fasting and being off her phone. She wrote that since I didn't have the wisdom and patience to wait for her call, she was going to 'teach me a lesson I'd never forget.' I would get my money back, but she would now only be sending it in small, slow drips.

"I wrote back that if Yom Kippur was the reason she hadn't returned my calls, then I profusely apologize. I also wrote that I'm the kind of guy who likes to finish things he's started, and actually wished I would have a beneficial business relationship with an honest person I consider like family. 'I plan to come to Vegas soon for another reason,' I wrote, 'and would be willing to stake much more money at that time.'"

"I know that *you* know this was all too late, and the damage was already done."

"Yes. And in the process of trying to sweet-talk my money back, I lost even more."

"What?"

"My integrity. I tried flattery on a woman who had no virtue. Then I tried to play on the sympathy of a woman who was born without a heart. When that didn't work, I resorted to threats. I wrote that if I didn't receive my money back immediately, I'd come to Vegas, find where she is, and not leave without it. I wrote that the only way she'd keep my money was over my dead body. I told her I'd at least had the good sense to make a copy of her driver's license, which I hadn't, and said that Dave is good friends with law enforcement, which he isn't. I ended by writing that I strongly advised her to not make me do anything we'd both regret. I knew it wouldn't work, because of the weakness I'd displayed in my prior interactions with her. But I did it to at least satisfy myself that I'd covered all the bases.

"It's not just the money, and it's not just about the specific amount. It's about *her* having it, and knowing she's wielding the power to keep it from me even though it's mine and I desperately need it. And it's also the knowledge that she has no fear that I will or can do anything to her, despite the threatening email. So, what I'm saying is that nothing works.

"I'm well aware of the detrimental things that happen to people who can't let go of stress. They're more prone to strokes, premature aging, and heart attacks. They can even gain weight, because stress produces cortisol, and cortisol's been shown to be detrimental to your metabolism. But how am I supposed to wipe this from my mind and let it go? Push a magic button? This has become an addiction and an obsession."

"You *can't* let it go or w*on't* let it go?"

"Can't, won't, whatever. The fact is, it's still here festering in me every single minute of every single day. You know, I never even thought of it until after I was back home in New York, and after I sent her the money. But one day, on a whim, I Googled her, not expecting to find anything. But lo and behold, it's all there. She's a publicly documented criminal, and I was horrified! All I would've had to do was Google her before this all started, and it would have saved me a lot of grief. I know I can't undo what's already done, but this whole situation is eating me alive."

"You know a lot more than you think you do."

"Yeah, just like a Monday-morning quarterback. I ignored every single red flag, did everything wrong, and said everything wrong. This was an absolute and total fuck-up. But what makes it even worse is that I feel this somehow *had* to happen. All throughout my life, whenever someone ripped me off or sold me something no good, my mother would always say, 'They saw you coming,' like I exuded the aura of a world-class schmuck someone could sell swampland in Florida to. I might as well be wearing a large sign proclaiming, 'I'm George. Shit on me.'

"And her evaluation of me didn't just refer to people who tried to sell me things. I'd be in a restaurant and the waitress would ignore me and take the orders of people who came a lot later than I did. Or I would order food, but everyone who came in later got their food first. If I'd relay my frustration to my mother, it ended up making it worse. Instead of the support I was looking for—you know, to have someone on my side—she would use that phrase or otherwise indicate I was a person who everyone knew they could shit on, even strangers."

"Why did you feel you *had* to relay these incidents to your mother?"

"That's a good question. I guess I was just wishing for something she couldn't give me. But anyway... when I broke all the rules but won a little anyway, with that first experience with the Poker Queen in Vegas, I was so glad I broke the mold. But there was a little voice inside me saying that I should've lost. And then I did."

"George, sometimes it takes a major fuck-up in order to learn an important lesson. In spite of your mother's opinion of you, I honestly don't believe there is any possibility that this will ever happen again. Or, I should say, that *you* will ever *allow* this to happen again."

"Of course not. I'll probably never go to Vegas again, and I'll definitely never post any ads again like I did. However, I guess I'll never really know 100 percent unless I were placed in that situation again. I told myself that until the day they close the lid on my coffin, this would *never* happen to me again. I also told myself that 500 dollars within the context of the rest of my life was minuscule. I'd use this as the catalyst to be ever vigilant, to 'respect' money, to not eat out often if I didn't have to, to always ask myself before buying something if I really needed it, and so on and so forth.

Successful people make many times more than this in a single hour.

"Sometimes I've indulged in really expensive clothes. Are the prices you have to pay to buy a designer suit worth it? Of course not. They might be *slightly* superior to a conventional suit. But I've voluntarily chosen to buy it…maybe because of the designer label, maybe because of the illusion. And I do get to wear it and enjoy it. But my point is that I know what the price is before I buy it, so the store owners aren't committing fraud. And different things are worth more and less to different people. The same with outrageously expensive restaurants. If the market couldn't bear it, they wouldn't still be in business. I figured I could chalk up my loss here to the same thing."

"Have you been ripped off before?"

"A multitude of times, Mildred. Fortunately, except in one other case, it wasn't for a substantial amount of money. But to this day, I still cringe when I revisit those instances in my mind. I almost wish that those situations would come up again, so that with the hindsight I now have, I'd immediately recognize it for what it is, and not let myself become a victim again. Someone could tell himself, and try to convince himself, that given the same situation, he'd never let what transpired happen again. But you don't really know for sure how you'd respond until it comes up. But as for the Poker Queen, I…oh, never mind."

"George, you had something you wanted to say."

"Yes. But you'd think I was totally irrational and crazy."

"George, if I haven't made it clear yet, I don't want you to hold back anything in therapy, regardless of what you think *I* might think. My job is not to make value judgments on whatever your thoughts or feelings are. Nor is it to judge you as a person. It's to explore your thoughts and feelings, to try to determine where they're coming from, and to deal with them in a way that isn't self-destructive. We all have irrational feelings, even feelings some people might call 'crazy,' from time to time. That's one of the features of being human. But there's a difference between having these feelings and reflexively acting out on these feelings in ways that can hurt us even more."

"How does one let go of these feelings, Mildred?"

"There isn't a 'one-size-fits-all' solution, George. Everyone's different. I once had a patient who was always full of anger and rage. I suggested he go to the gym and run on the treadmill until he was exhausted and out of breath. I advised another one with similar anger issues to make believe the punching bag at the gym was the person he despised. Both of these guys invariably felt better afterwards, because they focused their rage in a positive manner...and got a great physical workout to boot. Their anger and rage would always dissipate.

"I can't tell you how many times patients, male and female, have felt guilty and even mortified about admitting something to me. It's usually in soft, hushed tones, as if they've just revealed a deep and dark secret. They're then shocked when I don't react with revulsion and scold them."

"Okay, then don't say you didn't insist I tell you." He dramatically paused. "I fantasize about that motherfucker being dead."

Mildred smiled. "So that was your deep, dark secret?"

"You mean you don't think I'm a bad person?"

"As I told you, George, I'm not here to judge your thoughts and feelings. Let's face it; that Poker Queen of yours is a piece of shit." They both chuckled. "That's my official diagnosis. I know you wish you could go back in time and do it all over again. But one of the laws of reality is that you cannot redo the past. You can learn from it, but you can't erase it and put something else there. By obsessing over it, it's like wishing that one plus one isn't two and that the Earth isn't round. Reality can be a bitch, George, but it isn't what you want it to be. It is what it is."

"Mildred, I agree with you that the Poker Queen is nothing but a piece of shit. But at the same time, I'm shocked that a renowned psychologist who is supposed to understand people and delve into their feelings, emotions, and contexts would offer such a blanket assessment. What if she were your patient?"

"The Poker Queen could never *be* my patient, George, because I could never help someone like that if she *were* my patient. No matter what a person has done, they must have a conscience to benefit from therapy. She never will, because she believes, or has convinced herself, that she's done nothing wrong. She not only hurts other people, but derives pleasure from doing so. And I'll even go a step further and say that her crimes are premeditated. In other words, she seeks out opportunities to hurt others. And as if *that* weren't enough, she throws religion into the mix as her 'proof' that she could do no wrong, as if her religion is some sort of magic suit of armor that would physically prevent it. This, George, is my definition of evil.

"George, I'm not here to tell people what they want to hear. I leave that to the self-help gurus. Don't get me wrong; some of them have some value and wisdom to impart. But for many it's just a business; just churn out the same 'believe in yourself,' 'positive mental attitude,' 'you can be anything you want to be' bullshit, and keep repackaging it to sell more merchandise.

"I once had a patient who wanted guidance on how to date women, so he bought a dating guru's tapes. But after he bought them, he started getting ads urging him to buy more of them—'Advanced Dating Techniques,' 'Advanced Seduction,' and on and on. It occurred to me that if the original set of tapes were actually successful at teaching men how to pick up women, they wouldn't need to buy any more tapes."

"Mildred, why is wanting revenge wrong?"

"Who said it is?"

"Everything you read about it says it's not only wrong but self-defeating."

"George, this is one of those issues in which it can be a good thing *or* a self-destructive thing, depending on the circumstances. If someone has wronged me but has made reparations, and is truly sorry and repentant, I can see forgiving that person. But when someone has hurt or tries to hurt an innocent person, then hurting or wanting to hurt that person back is understandable. It becomes destructive when there's no possibility of you receiving justice but you let the situation consume you anyway, as you've done regarding the Poker Queen. You live and *re*live the situation every day. It's blown way out of proportion in your mind. It immobilizes you from doing constructive things in the present and future, because not all of your attention is on the *now*; it's on the past. You can function, but not at full capacity.

"It's like a car pulling a huge load up a steep mountain road. It makes it, but with great difficulty. The object of your hate and rage then 'owns' you. You've granted them enormous power over you, because you've allowed them to victimize you for eternity. You've been holding onto this shit long after the encounter was over. This enormous power is more than she even thought she possessed. And if by some dispensation, she would've been able to track your mind, it would make her that much happier…because the more pain an evil person can inflict, the happier they are.

"George, you know how I feel about many sayings that are passed down. But there's one I love, and it's one of my favorites: 'Why let an evil person live rent-free inside your head?' At times revenge *is* possible. But you have to ask yourself what the cost is. By sending her threatening emails, you leave *yourself* open to getting in trouble. And of course, a person like that would have no qualms about lying in order to enhance how bad it already looks. Sometimes people do get 'even,' for lack of a better word. But they end up spending their life in prison, effectively throwing their own life away in the process. Other times the person dies before we could've ever gotten revenge. They continue to victimize us even from the grave."

Mildred paused and looked at her watch. "George, I'd like to continue our discussion next week. Would next Monday at the same time be too far ahead for you?"

"Next Monday would be perfect."

"And if you need to talk for any reason before that time, please feel free to call."

"Thanks so much. I really appreciate it. But I wish I could do something for you, too."

"Well, actually there *is* something you could do. If you don't have anything planned on Saturday evening, Jim and I are having an informal cocktail party, and we'd love for you to come over to play for us."

"I'd love to. That's the least I could do."

"Great. The party starts around 7:00 p.m. See you Saturday."

CHAPTER TWO

George had been playing the piano at Mildred and Jim's party that Saturday for a while when a slim, blue-collar gentleman approached. "That's beautiful," he said. "You really tickle those ivories. I always had a secret wish I could play, but to tell you the truth, I never had the discipline. Can you play 'My Way'?"

"Sure," said George, and immediately launched into it. The gentleman started singing along. "Excuse my singing. I ain't no Sinatra. My wife always tells me I sound like someone's torturing a cat. But I love music, and I can't help singing along. Tony Blangiardo." He extended his hand for a warm handshake.

"George Sistern."

"A pleasure to meet you, George." During the handshake, Tony had slipped a ten-dollar bill into his palm.

"Oh no, Tony. That's not necessary. I was more than happy to play that for you."

Tony waved him off. "Any friend of Mildred and Jim is a friend of mine."

Mildred then appeared. She and Tony exchanged a warm hug and a kiss on both cheeks. "I see you've met George," she said.

"Yes, I've already had the pleasure."

Tony Blangiardo was fifty-six years old, lived in Bay Ridge, and owned a chop shop and auto salvage yard in Ozone Park. Cars would come in and would be crushed for metal. He'd been married to Maria, his high school sweetheart, for thirty-one years. He had one daughter, Gina, who was twenty-one. He loved his wife and daughter fiercely; they were his greatest values.

He had worked his way up in the mob since he became a made man at nineteen, and had ties all the way to the upper echelons. He was a quiet and friendly man, and neighbors had only good things to say about him. He would anonymously shovel their cars when there were snowstorms, help old ladies cross the street or lift their heavy bags at the supermarket. He gave to various charities, and even opened his home to homeless people on Thanksgiving. He was quick with a smile and a joke.

But beneath the exterior was a side of him that he mostly kept hidden from his family. He had a violent temper, and couldn't tolerate cruelty or injustice against the weak or innocent. In instances when he heard about people who'd done terrible things, his auto salvage yard would be put to use for purposes other than crushing cars. This is how some people completely disappeared off the face of the Earth. And if you were one of those people, there was nowhere in the world you could hide.

At the end of the evening, Tony invited George to come over to his home in Bay Ridge the following week. "I'd love to," replied George.

"But you've got to promise me one thing."

"What's that?"

"Come with an appetite."

George came over the following week and met Tony's wife, Maria, and his daughter, Gina. There were about twenty other people there, and Tony introduced George to everyone. There was a truckload of food and desserts all spread out, buffet-style. "Please help yourself, George," said Tony. "And don't be shy here. *Mangia.* One thing about us you gotta know; if you don't eat enough, we get personally insulted."

George ate so much that he was stuffed, and Tony eventually responded, "You know what, George? We really like you, but if you're gonna be part of the family, you're gonna have to improve in one area."

"What's that?"

"You eat like a bird." With that, Tony slapped him on the back and laughed heartily.

When people started clearing out, Tony asked George to hang around. "So how do you know Mildred and Jim?" he asked.

"Someone I know saw I was very depressed and recommended that I go see Mildred."

"I don't mean to pry, but do you have personal emotional issues that you have to deal with, or was someone trying to hurt you?"

"Both. And as for hurting me, someone didn't *try* to hurt me. She did."

"Did this have anything to do with romance?"

"No. Nothing like that. I met a con artist who scammed me out of money."

"I see. If you don't have to be anywhere, I'd like to have a little talk with you when the guests leave."

"It's okay. I can hang around."

After the last guest left, Tony asked George to follow him into the den. They sat facing one another on two plush leather sofas. "George, if anything I ask you is none of my business, just tell me, okay?" George nodded. "Mildred's a remarkable woman, the smartest and most caring woman I've ever met…next to my wife, of course." Tony chuckled. "I know that getting your brain shrunk can be very valuable and all, but sometimes there are practical solutions to problems as well. But before I ask you what happened—and like I said, you don't have to tell me if you don't want to—I'll tell you how *I* met Mildred and Jim.

"About three years ago, Gina was meeting two of her girlfriends in Little Italy. You usually can't get a parking spot on Mulberry Street, so Gina would park on Mercer Street. It's kind of deserted there, so you always have to worry about someone breaking into your car if they don't steal it. But Gina would usually take a chance, because it was much easier to park there.

"Anyway, it's about 11:00 p.m., and all of a sudden, three motherfuckers appear out of nowhere and start beating the shit out of her. They had ripped her clothes off and were about to rape her when suddenly a good Samaritan who lived in one of the buildings there heard her screaming, ran outside, and blew all three of those bastards away. The good Samaritan was Jim. By this time, Mildred had rushed out, and Jim told her to go inside and get blankets. She rushed inside, got the blankets to cover her up, then they took her inside. As you can imagine, after having just been savagely beaten by three strangers, and now going into the home of two strangers, Mildred had to use all her persuasive powers to convince her everything was okay now, and that they weren't there to hurt her.

"Mildred asked Gina where she lived, and she said she lived in Bay Ridge with me and Maria. They ask Gina for our number so they could call us, and when a different number comes up and I hear Gina weeping in the background, me and Maria start freaking out. Meanwhile, Mildred's trying to explain to me what happened and is trying to calm us down. Gina was bruised up, has a black eye, but nothing's broken. She then gives me her address, and me and Maria drive over there.

"When we arrived, Mildred and Jim did everything they could to calm us down, and assure us that everything was okay. Gina was banged up and traumatized but not seriously hurt. Mildred gave us hot chocolate, and made us feel at home.

"I take out my checkbook and offer them five thousand dollars. They turn it down, but I insist. They still refuse to take it. They say this isn't something people do for money. It's something any decent person would want to do for someone in trouble. They said that the only reward they wanted was to know that Gina was okay. And right then and there, I told Jim and Mildred that we consider them a part of the family, and I love them like my own wife and daughter. And I also told them if they ever needed me for any reason, or if anyone ever tried to hurt them or one of their friends or family, they had to promise to tell me, and that person would never hurt another person again."

George then told Tony what he had told Mildred. Tony listened intently, and asked a lot of questions so as to be filled in on all the details. George had had both of the numbers she had given him, but had thrown them out in an attempt to achieve closure. Yet the situation kept haunting him. He'd awaken in the middle of the night screaming obscenities and pounding his pillow in rage. Then one of her numbers turned up by accident, and he felt he shouldn't throw it out. But now he felt guilty that he threw out the other one. Maybe that was the "better" number.

"Don't you worry," said Tony. "It's a small world. She'll be very easy to find." And he was right. Unlisted numbers, phony addresses, fake names and IDs all made no difference to a man with all the right connections.

"Listen, Tony, five hundred dollars and change is not an enormous amount of money, and it's certainly insignificant compared to what happened to Gina. And to be very honest with you, I have to take responsibility for letting this happen. I ignored every single red flag and allowed this woman to rip me off anyway. I should have gift wrapped her the money on a silver platter."

"You're right, George. Five hundred dollars is not a major sum of money. But it was enough to fuck up your brain, and torture you every day to the point that you had to go see a shrink over it. We all do stupid things, George, and sometimes people who are smart learn from it and never make the same mistake again. But you're torturing yourself, because even though you know you'd never let this happen to you again, you don't really know, because you won't ever place yourself in that predicament again. And meanwhile, in your mind, you can see that fucking woman laughing at you and congratulating herself. Am I right?"

"Yeah."

"The actual amount of money is not the issue, George. It could have been any amount…any amount she could get away with swindling. Are you naïve enough to think you were her only mark? And marks with means were relieved of a lot more than 500 dollars. I can assure you of that. Whether a given amount of money is a large sum or not is all relative. To us, 500 dollars is not a lot of money. But in some Third World countries, some of those dirt-poor people don't even make 500 dollars in a year. 500 dollars to them would be like winning the fucking lottery."

"I know," said George. "Mildred said the same thing."

"George, Mildred is a fantastic woman, and I've heard she's an incredible therapist. She can tell you all the right words, but there's one practical thing she *can't* do for you. And that's get you your money back. Now, I ain't no shrink or nothing. But I think that whatever words of wisdom she gives you, you ain't gonna let this go. Am I right?" George nodded. "And I know that even though you know that if the same situation came up again, you wouldn't let what happened to you happen again, you're still not going to achieve closure unless you get your money back or found out someone else permanently took care of the Poker Queen problem. Am I right about that too?"

"Yeah."

"So, in that case, I want to get you your money back. Do I have your permission?"

"You're not going to physically hurt her?"

"No. As long as she doesn't try to physically have me or my friends hurt. I'm just going to get you your money back."

"Okay."

Four days after Tony spoke with George, he gave him a call. "Just as I suspected. She's still in Vegas. She didn't go nowhere. Her son's facing time for bank robbery, and she's been lying her ass off trying to get him off. She usually plays at the Aria, sometimes at the Rio, but it don't matter. We got her picture in all the casinos on the Strip and downtown. I'll have my guys gambling at the same table as her. And we'll also be paying off the pit bosses and the eyes in the sky to watch her every move and have everything videotaped."

Tony sent his lieutenant Carmine to Vegas. The purpose was to participate in any poker games the Poker Queen played in. He started with the Aria, sought out the floor manager, showed him a picture of the Poker Queen, and asked if he recognized her. He said, "Oh yes, she's in here often, in the poker room. And if she wins, she plays the slots and loses everything she won."

Carmine slipped him a hundred-dollar bill and a card with his cell phone number. "I'd appreciate if you tell me whenever you see her."

"Sure, no problem," said the floor manager.

The next day, Carmine got a call while he was having dinner. The Poker Queen had just sat down at the table in the poker room at the Aria. Carmine rushed over, spotted her, and sat down at a vacant seat at the same table. After about an hour, the Poker Queen was up about 200 dollars and decided to cash out. She went to the table where the players cash in their chips, and Carmine approached her. "Miss, can I have a word with you, please? I've been watching you and I just gotta say…damn, you're good. It's obvious you're not one of those typical tourists who don't know what they're doing."

"Thank you. I've been playing for many years, know the game inside out, and I'm also a master of psychology. Some people know how to play the game, but they don't know how to read people, don't know when to bluff. That's why they call me the Poker Queen. I've sat in on tournaments with some of the biggest names, and beaten them all. No one intimidates me, and I hate to lose."

"I can tell that. You have that kind of aura about you."

"One time I was losing badly, had all the wrong cards, but remained cool and calm. I was playing this champion, and he fell for it. Almost everyone else shows it on their face, but psychology is just as important as technique. I ended up beating him."

"Holy shit. I'd give anything to be like you, but to be very honest, I'm a lousy player. I get cleaned out every time I come to Vegas."

"Maybe you need a pro playing for you."

"Is this something you'd really consider?"

"Sure. Just put up the money, we'll split the winnings fifty-fifty, and I'll show you how it feels to win. I'd need a place to stay, though, as I live too far from the Strip. This way, I could get some sleep and then get straight back to the tables right away."

Carmine asked her where she wanted to stay, and she said it'd be more convenient for her to stay at the Aria, since that was where she usually played. So Carmine paid for a three-night stay at the Aria for the Poker Queen. Fortunately, she wasn't particular about food, and didn't have any interest in going to restaurants. It was too time-consuming, she said, and would take away time that could be better spent at the tables.

So Carmine satisfied her appetite with fried chicken and Chinese food.

Carmine only gave the Poker Queen about three or four hundred dollars at a time. After the three days, she had basically broken even, which meant that Carmine was behind. He had paid for her hotel room and food, as well as for his own, not to mention the round-trip airfare to get to Vegas in the first place. And whenever the Poker Queen won, she would ask for a tip, which Carmine always gave her. When Carmine said that he really had to get back to New York, the Poker Queen asked why. "You're a good player and all; I ain't gonna deny that," he replied. "But breaking even ain't really gonna do nothin' for me. I gotta pay the airfare, the hotel for me and you, food…"

"Listen," said the Poker Queen. "I told you that if you really want me to win for you, I have to have more money to play with. In that last game, when I won 500 dollars, it would've been over 5,000 dollars if I were able to bet 1,000 dollars on some of the hands, rather than three or four hundred. The more money you bet on a winning hand, the more you make."

"Yeah, I know what you're sayin'," said Carmine, "but I ain't no rich man. I'm just a working stiff. But

I'll tell you what; I'll tell my boss about you. He'd be able to put up some real money."

"Tell him I'll show him what a pro can do for him. Who *is* your boss, by the way?"

"His name is Angelo Rutollo."

"Who is he?"

"You've never heard of him?"

"Should I have?"

"He's only one of the most successful real estate developers in the country. He owns condo developments all over Nevada, Utah, and Arizona. He also purchases residential homes, renovates them into mint condition, flips them, and makes huge profits. Unfortunately, he doesn't have any more than a rudimentary knowledge of casino games, so he mostly just plays the roulette wheel, slots, stuff like that. And obviously, he loses most of the time. But at least he's comped for almost everything.

"He always has a suite waiting for him at the Wynn, dines in the finest restaurants, gets to see the headliners, and always gets ringside seats whenever there's a championship boxing match. He also gets fitted for custom-made Brioni suits, gets massages, the whole works. And of course, he never has to worry about the inconvenience and discomfort of flying into town on a regular airline. He's flown in whenever they can get him to come. He wouldn't trust himself at games like blackjack and poker, however, and has often said he wished he could have a pro play for him."

"Well, you bring him to me, and he'll see the difference between an average tourist who doesn't know what they're doing and a pro."

Tony arrived in town several days later, and Carmine informed him of his name change. Carmine had told him that the Poker Queen usually played at the Aria, so he booked a room there and went upstairs to freshen up. Carmine then arranged for the three of them to meet in a lounge at the hotel. Spotting the Poker Queen arriving twenty minutes later, Carmine introduced them, then excused himself.

"You can call me Angie," said Tony. "So, Carmine tells me you're quite skilled at poker."

"'Quite skilled' is an understatement," said the Poker Queen. "I'm one of the best in the world, a lifelong student of the game, a master of psychology, and I hate to lose. If you stick with me, I'll show you how it feels to win, and to win big. You put up the money, we'll split the winnings fifty-fifty, and the more you put up, the more you'll win."

"Sounds great," said Tony. "That is, if you are who you say you are, and do what you say you can do. You do right by me, I'll do right by you. But please forgive me for not being as excited as maybe I should be. I'm not referring to you, but I *have* been burned in the past."

"Well, let me tell you something, Angie. I happen to be a devoutly religious Jew, and one of the tenets of my religion is to always live by the highest ethical standards. I would never, nor *could* ever, do anything dishonest. That would be totally against my religion. That's my proof. I also have a saying: 'My word is my bond.' That means when you're dealing with someone like me, my word is as good as any contract or signed document. Honesty is my greatest virtue, and that's how I live my life."

"I never meant to question your honesty, ma'am. I was just saying that I've been burned in the past, and one can never be too careful."

"I understand. But with me, you'd never have anything to worry about." She glanced at her watch. "There's a game starting in the poker room in fifteen minutes. Why don't you join me?"

"I'd like to, but I need to go to my room to take care of a few things first." Although Tony usually stayed at the Wynn, he had booked a room for five days at the Aria this time in order to be closer to the Poker Queen, whom he also booked a room for.

"No problem. I can start without you. Just join me there when you're finished doing what you have to do. I'll need some cash to start with, though."

"How much would you like?"

"Five thousand dollars would be good."

"Listen, Celestial. I've done alright for myself. But I grew up dirt poor, so I know what it feels like. One thing my mother, may she rest in peace, always stressed to me is to respect money, and never waste it. Because no matter how much you have, it could always be gone just like that."

"Well, in Vegas, that might be true with something like the slots or the roulette wheel, but with poker you're not betting against the house, which always has the advantage. Poker is a game of skill, and the greatest players *consistently* win."

"I understand what you're saying, but that's a little bit above my comfort level."

"Okay, I'll tell you what. Let's start with a thousand. Here," she said, and handed him her driver's license.

Tony met up with the Poker Queen about twenty minutes later, and was allowed to sit right next to her. "Give me my license," she said, and Tony handed it over. In about half an hour, she had turned 1,000 dollars into 7,000 dollars and cashed out. "See?" she said. "Do you believe me now? If I had had 5,000 dollars to work with, we could've made over 30,000 thousand dollars by now."

They then went to the cashier to cash the chips. Taxes were deducted from the winnings, Tony took his 1,000 dollars back and gave half of what was left to the Poker Queen. "How about a tip?" she asked, so Tony handed her a hundred-dollar bill.

The next day, Tony and Carmine met with the Poker Queen at one of the fast-food joints in the hotel, where Tony bought everyone lunch. "Okay, you saw what I could do," said the Poker Queen. "Let's go back to the same place tonight, but with more money to work with."

"What did you have in mind?" asked Tony.

"5,000 dollars."

"Okay."

"But how about you letting me hold onto 1,000 dollars until we play?"

"Why don't I just give you the whole 5,000 dollars when we meet in the poker room tonight?"

"I'm trying to establish trust between us. Didn't I let you hold onto my license yesterday?"

"Yes, but that's because I let you walk off with my 1,000 dollars."

"But I didn't disappear, did I?"

"Okay, here you go," said Tony, and handed over 1,000 dollars.

"See you in the poker room at 7:00 p.m.," said the Poker Queen, and left.

"Are you crazy, Tony?" said Carmine. "She could just disappear now."

"I don't think so," said Tony. "Not in this case. I think she'll show up to prove her 'honesty,' because she'll be thinking of how much she could win with my 5,000 dollars and wouldn't want to jeopardize it."

At 7:00 p.m., Tony arrived at the poker room. Celestial was waiting for him. "Can I have my thousand dollars?" asked Tony.

"Why don't we add this to the 5,000 dollars?" asked Celestial. "Any winning hand with 6,000 dollars would make us so much more than working with 1,000 dollars less."

Tony said, "Okay."

In about forty minutes, the Poker Queen had lost everything. "Nice meeting you," said Tony, and started to walk out.

"Angie," Celestial called out, and Tony stopped. "Please, you mustn't be discouraged. There's no such thing as winning all the time. The greatest players in the world have all lost from time to time. It's unavoidable. The best player in the world can lose to a common tourist if he has a terrible hand and the tourist has a great hand. But what separates the amateurs from the pros is that the pros win consistently. Even if they're losing to begin with, if they keep playing it eventually turns around. In poker, skill always trumps luck long-range. Trust me, and have confidence in me. Come on, let's play again tomorrow night, and I'll show you how it feels to win."

"I can't," said Tony. "I've already bought tickets to a show."

"No problem," said the Poker Queen. "You don't have to be there."

"I don't think so," said Tony. "I wouldn't feel comfortable with that."

"Look, I'll take a picture of the table before and after, and I'll let you know everything that happens."

"Alright," said Tony. "How much do you want?"

"10,000 dollars," said the Poker Queen.

Tony then handed over 10,000 dollars in hundred-dollar bills. When the Poker Queen left, he then gave the pit boss 200 dollars to inform him of what happened in the game later. After an hour of playing that night, the Poker Queen had turned 10,000 dollars into 50,000 dollars, but didn't take a picture of the table. Nor did she inform Tony of what had happened.

The next morning, Tony called the Poker Queen and said he wanted to meet her for lunch. At noon they met in front of another fast-food place. "So what happened?" asked Tony.

"Listen, I was up by a lot, and I had to bluff on one hand. If I had won that hand, I would've made us a fortune. But one cannot guess right 100 percent of the time."

"Didn't you tell me you'd keep me informed of everything that went on?"

"Yes, but I was so into the game and concentrating so much that I completely forgot. Poker is kind of like chess in that the great players always think ahead and analyze all the contingencies. Sometimes, the difference between losing and winning big comes down to guessing right on one hand. Like I told you the other day, the greatest players in the world all lose from time to time."

"Yes, but this is the second time in a row that you've lost my money."

"Angie, haven't even the greatest basketball teams lost two games in a row once in a while? You can never judge a team—or a poker player, for that matter—over the results of just two games. Listen, there's going to be a big game at the Rio in two days. The buy-in is twenty-five grand."

"Are you crazy?" said Tony.

"Wait a minute, let me finish," said the Poker Queen. "Do you know what the winner will walk away with? 100,000 dollars. That's four times the buy-in."

"Yeah, but you could lose the whole 25,000 dollars also."

"Look, Angie, someone's gonna win, and that someone can be me. No one's ever achieved great things who hasn't dreamed big. But this isn't throwing darts at a board blindfolded. I'm as good as anyone in that tournament, and I've beaten some of the top players in the world. This is our time, Angie. Trust me, and have confidence in me."

"Okay," said Tony. "Let's do it. But first, I want you to let me hold onto 5,000 dollars of *your* money."

"5,000 dollars?! Don't you trust me, Angie?"

"Didn't I let you hold on to 1,000 dollars of *my* money?"

"Yes. But I didn't run away with it. I showed up, didn't I? But 5,000 dollars is five times as much."

"And the buy-in is 25,000 dollars, which is five times 5,000 dollars."

"But don't you trust me, Angie?"

"Let me hold on to the 5,000 dollars so we can *establish* trust. If you do, then I'll return the 5,000 dollars to you before the tournament, and pay the 25,000 dollar buy-in."

"I couldn't afford to lose it."

"Well, if that's what you think will happen, then I think we should just go our separate ways. It was nice meeting you." Tony then turned and walked away.

The Poker Queen rushed after him. "Okay," she said, and handed Tony 5,000 dollars.

Two days later, Tony met the Poker Queen at the designated place in the Rio, and handed her the 5,000 dollars back. "So, have we established trust now?" he asked.

"Yes. I'm sorry," she said. "It's just that it was a lot of money."

Tony then paid the 25,000 dollar buy-in and took his place next to the Poker Queen at the table. Over four hours, the Poker Queen prevailed and won the tournament. Taxes were then taken out of the winnings, Tony took back his 25,000 dollars, split the remainder with the Poker Queen, and gave her a 1,000 dollar tip.

Tony then said he had business to attend to back in New York. The Poker Queen said that in two months, the World Series of Poker would be held, with the chance to win three million dollars. Tony said he'd return at that time.

Over the next two months, the Poker Queen blew her entire winnings on poker, the slots, and legal fees for her son. About three weeks before the tournament, she called Tony. "Angie, the tournament is starting soon. The buy-in is 60,000 dollars, but the winner will take home three million. Let's do it."

"How about contributing a little to the buy-in?"

"But I don't have anything, Angie."

"You won thousands of dollars in the tournament at the Rio two months ago, and you don't have anything?"

"I know, but my son was accused of something he's totally innocent of, and the legal fees I've had to pay ate up all my money."

"Listen, sixty grand is a lot of money. You're asking me to incur a huge risk."

"But the winner will take home three million. This is not a pipe dream. Didn't you see me win the last tournament? If being too afraid to risk sixty grand kept you from winning three million dollars, you'd be kicking yourself forever."

"Okay, Celestial, you want me to shell out sixty grand? Send me your wedding ring as collateral."

"Oh God, Angie, I could never do that. That's from my late husband. It's fourteen-carat gold and is worth 25,000 dollars. Why would you ever want me to risk losing something so precious to me?"

"I asked you just to send me some cash, but apparently you have nothing left. But somehow when I ask you to send me your wedding ring as collateral, all of a sudden all the trust I thought we'd established is gone. I'm sorry, Celestial. If you don't trust me with the wedding ring, I'm not laying out sixty grand, which *I* couldn't afford to lose. Have a nice day."

"Wait. Okay, I'll send it, but do you swear you'll then come to Vegas with the 60,000 dollars plus my wedding ring?"

"Celestial, you made it very clear to me that your word was your bond, and I believed you. So now I'm saying the same thing to you, and asking you to believe *me*."

"Okay."

Tony then gave Celestial the post office box of an acquaintance, and Celestial express-mailed the wedding ring. The acquaintance then delivered the ring to Tony. A few days later, Celestial called Tony to make sure the ring had arrived. "Yes, I got it," said Tony. "By the way, do you happen to remember someone named George Sistern?"

"Yes, we met about three years ago."

"Well, he happens to be a dear friend of mine, and he told me that he sent you 500 dollars to play poker with, and you said you would mail him 50 percent of your profits."

"I remember. But then he called me a thief, and I was so insulted, I figured he didn't deserve to make a profit on it. But believe it or not, I was just going to send the money back to him."

"What address were you going to send it to?"

"Hold on a minute. I'll check."

When the Poker Queen came back to the phone, she said that she couldn't find George's address. "If you don't have his address, how would you have sent him the money?" asked Tony.

"I didn't say I didn't have it. I said I misplaced it."

"No problem," said Tony. "Just mail 500 dollars cash to the same address you mailed the ring to, and I'll see that George gets it."

"Okay, but do you swear that you'll then come back to Vegas before the tournament with my ring and the 60,000-dollar buy-in?"

"Celestial, I live my life by the same code of values and honesty that you do. And my word is *my* bond."

A few days later, Celestial called Tony to make sure the 500 dollars got there. "Yes, it did," said Tony. "And by the way, George sends his regards."

"So now we're ready for the tournament in another two days?"

"Well, so here's the thing now. Do you remember when I was in Vegas with you and I said I couldn't join you at the Aria because I had tickets for a show that night? And you said you'd take pictures of the table before and after and give me 50 percent of the winnings?"

"Yes," she said with confusion. "I already told you I lost that night."

"I remember what you told me. But there's a problem with that, because before I went to the show, I went to the casino's security and paid them to give me a report on everything that happened that night. The pit boss said you won forty grand. That would mean you owe me a lot of money. If what you say is true, that means Alan's a liar, and I'll have to show up in Vegas with my lawyer and call the police over to the casino, so all of us can check the videotapes to find out for ourselves what exactly happened."

"No, don't do that. He was telling the truth. Listen, my son happens to be in a lot of trouble, and is accused of something he's completely innocent of. I've been having to spend thousands in legal fees to try to clear him. I owed my attorney a lot of money, and he said if he didn't get it, he'd drop the case. I couldn't risk that happening."

"What about all of this indicates your honesty?"

"I understand what you mean, Angie, and I'm sorry. I was under so much pressure, and I couldn't think clearly. I couldn't take the risk of the lawyer dropping the case. And I was going to pay you back. I swear."

"I'll tell you what," said Tony. "Just mail me my cut, and I'll see you in Vegas in two weeks with your ring and the 60,000-dollar buy-in."

"But I just told you, Angie, I don't have it."

"Well, as soon as you do, let me know and I'll be happy to send your ring back." With that, Tony hung up.

The Poker Queen kept calling, but this time Tony wouldn't answer the phone. She would leave frantic messages after she heard the beep. Then Tony had her number blocked. He called George to say he had a little present for him, but would like to give it to him in person. Could he come over for dinner over the weekend? When George came over, Tony handed him an envelope. He opened it, and inside were five 100-dollar bills. His eyes widened, and his mouth opened.

"I could've mailed it to you," said Tony, "but I wanted to see the look on your face."

"Is it really from whom I'm thinking?" asked George.

Tony just smiled and nodded.

The next day they both went to a dealer in the Diamond District, had the ring appraised, and sold it for 18,000 dollars, which Tony then gave to George. "Gee, Tony," he said, "she only stole 500 dollars from me."

"Consider it interest and dividends for pain and suffering. And besides, when I was in Vegas, she stole my money, too. George, it's not morally wrong to steal from a thief who steals from you, just as it's not immoral to hurt or kill someone who tries to hurt or kill us or a loved one. Can we now consider this enormous load you've been carrying around for several years finally lifted?"

"Yes," said George, and the two men held each other in a long embrace.

"But if you want to pay me back, there's one thing you can do for me if you want."

"What's that?" asked George.

"You can play 'My Way' for me again at Mildred's next party." The two men laughed. "And maybe Mildred should pay me a commission for helping her out with some of her patients."

"You've got a point," said George. "She could designate you as her assistant." Both of them laughed again.

* * *

On Monday, George went back to Mildred for another session. "You look a lot better today," said Mildred.

"I feel a lot better, too." George then told Mildred that his Poker Queen problem was permanently solved, and got her caught up on the story. He assured her that he didn't volunteer the information to Tony, but that Tony had specifically asked for it.

"Well, I'm glad you achieved closure on this," she replied, "but I hope you realize that the way to measure one's progress—or transcendence, I suppose, for lack of a better word—is what he or she does to not get into a situation like you did in the first place. But if someone *does* make a mistake—and we're only human, which means that all of us will make mistakes—the question is, 'What's the best and most productive way to deal with it? What's the best way not to immobilize myself in the present? And what can I do to make sure it never happens again?'

"Yes, you lucked out here and got your money back. But imagine if Tony had tracked her down and she was already dead; if you didn't know about it, that means she'd have literally been victimizing you from the grave. Do you really want to give someone that much power over you? George, you are more than your problems, and you are more than your mistakes. When something happens, the law of reality states that you cannot alter it. It's already happened. At that stage, you can either use the experience for or against you. But you can't erase it and do it over again.

"Now, does that mean you can't learn from it, and that it can't help you make sure you never get yourself into a similar situation again? Of course not. That's what life and growth is all about. We make mistakes, we learn from them, and we grow. I know you've heard the cliché that we learn more from our failures than from our successes, but it's true. Our failures create an imbalance. In other words, we become unhappy. We know we made a mistake or that something didn't work. The question is, what do we do about it?

"You had a very bad experience with a specimen of the lowest form of human scum. If it weren't for Tony, you never would've been able to achieve justice. But what was your alternative? What would've been the upside for you of letting this cancer fester in your system interminably, and to continue to grow and wreak havoc upon your well-being, both mental and physical? Even if you had gone back to Vegas and won a jackpot, you still would've been thinking of the 500 dollars that piece of shit scammed you out of. She would have still 'owned' you, and you would have still been her 'prisoner.' Why? Because you based your happiness on either getting your money back from her, or on her destruction. Again I ask, do you really want to give her such power?

"I was just reading the other day about how some of the most successful businessmen in history have gone on to achieve astounding success only after suffering *two* bankruptcies. That means they fucked up not once but *twice*. Think about it. Now, it says a lot about their perseverance and resiliency. But the bottom line is, it was only money. And money can come and go, dependent on your ability to make it and to know what to do with it once you get it.

"And if you *do* make a mistake, you cut your losses and learn what you can from it. In this case, you develop an emotional firewall, like with computers. Nothing teaches us, George, like experience and cold, hard reality. Your rational side knew that her intention was to relieve you of your money. But your fantasy side planted a tiny question in the back of your head: 'What if it could really happen?' Was it theoretically possible that she would win money and then send your share of the winnings to you? Yes. But now take out the word 'theoretically' and again ask yourself the same question. I think you know the answer; but you wouldn't have really known for sure unless you had experienced the pain that results when one places fantasy above reality. And, I might add, the more self-esteem a person has, the less likely they are to make such errors of judgment.

"Most of the pain that results from the consequences of our mistakes is self-imposed. In instances where we're not physically hurt or the victim of a violent crime, we often hurt ourselves more than our perpetrators could have. We fuck up our *own* minds. Someone can rob you of money, but they can't plant something in your brain unless you allow them to. You allowed yourself to plant all this toxic poison in your brain, and allowed it to grow. What's the antidote? It's to be found in the saying that I already recited for you: 'Why let an evil person live rent-free inside your head?'

"You know, George, one of the symptoms of dementia is forgetting things. But there's one kind of situation in which that's a *good* thing, and that's when you refuse to think about evil people. Maybe we should call it 'convenient amnesia.' You know, there was once a story in the news about a monster who brutally killed a woman's daughter. He was sentenced to life without parole. After the necessary grieving process, and after all the rage, there came a time to put him behind her. Did that mean she would forget about her daughter? Never. She'll be in her heart until the day she dies. But to continue to focus on the monster who took her from her would allow him to continue victimizing her.

"She decided to no longer think of him. 'He's not worth my thoughts,' she said. 'He's not worth my time.' The Poker Queen is not worth your thoughts, George. And even if that scum, or any other scum, is still alive, if you wipe someone like that out of your mind, then in essence they no longer exist. And if they no longer exist, they can no longer hurt you."

CHAPTER THREE

A week later, George returned to Mercer Street for another session. "Mildred, even if you didn't know Tony, you helped me, because you gave me permission to fuck up. I was so embarrassed to admit the stupid mistakes I made."

"Because you thought I'd pass judgment?"

"That's right."

"Everyone passes judgment, whether they're aware of it or not. One of the most famous self-help gurus proclaims there's no such thing as a bad outcome or performance. In other words, a piano student who can't play two right notes in a row or keep a steady beat hasn't actually delivered a bad performance; he's produced a result. This inspirational bullshit appeases the untalented, the lazy, and the masses, and helps sell books. But it is never denounced for what it is, because however misleading statements like this are, there are elements of truth in them. And that's why these gurus can get away with them."

"What do you mean?"

"Almost everyone can improve at things that are important to them. And yes, mistakes can act as learning tools *if* we learn from them and initiate specific actions to lessen their recurrence. But if we don't distinguish between a kid banging out 'Chopsticks' and Vladimir Horowitz performing a Chopin mazurka, this means we have no means of objectively passing judgment on a work of art. A monkey sticking its tail in a container of paint, then splashing it on a canvas, is as great a work of art as a painting by Rembrandt, according to people like this guru, because art is unquantifiable. The simple truth is, George, Michael Jordan was a better basketball player than you and I could ever be, and Novak Djokovic a better tennis player. This isn't opinion but cold, hard fact. But do you *want* to be as good as Jordan or Djokovic?"

"I wouldn't complain if I were, but don't care that I'm not."

"Why not?"

"Because basketball and tennis aren't my top priorities in life."

"What are?"

"I'd feel uncomfortable telling you."

"Because you think if you did, you'd feel inferior if you couldn't measure up to the top people at whatever it is you want to be great at."

"Something like that."

"George, you're right. I *would* pass judgment on things you did. If you played the piano for me, I would naturally form an opinion as to the quality of your performance. My memory would bring me back to other performances I heard of the same piece, and whether consciously or unconsciously, I would be comparing. This doesn't mean my assessments would always be accurate, and it doesn't mean I wouldn't think you could improve, even to the point of being able to take an objectively poor performance and eventually make it great. It just means I would've at that point formed an opinion. But think about this. There are great masters who can hear a young pianist and think of a million things he could be doing better, but at the same time want him as a student. Why? Because they recognize the raw talent...the ability and creativity bursting at the seams and wanting to express itself, but that just needs direction, knowledge, guidance, and a means of harnessing all this energy and passion that's ready to explode. The same can be said about young painters, dancers, singers, actors and writers.

"And even if I did judge your performance, I wouldn't pass judgment on the validity of your feelings, because feelings aren't right or wrong, George.

It's how we *deal* with them that's important. So, I *would* pass judgment on how you chose to deal with your feelings. Aside from any mistakes you made in regard to the Poker Queen, the biggest mistake is what you did to *yourself* long after your interaction with her was over. And the torture and flagellation that you inflicted upon yourself was worse than whatever that scum did to you. But just like an objectively poor piano performance, the objectively poor and self-destructive thoughts and actions that we allow to eat us alive can be similarly improved."

"How?"

"By having or acquiring self-esteem. When this is possessed, it's impervious to any mistakes we make, and it's impervious to the actions of others. That's one of the great things about it. For those who possess it, it's a given—an irreducible primary—and cannot be taken away from us by anyone else or by any circumstance."

"I think I understand what you're saying. But what about people who don't have it? How do you acquire it? I went to a seminar once by one of those famous self-help gurus, and he told everyone in the audience that they had to look in the mirror every morning and chant, 'I am great! I am great! I am a winner!'"

"That's total bullshit. Chanting a mantra isn't worth the breath it takes to chant it unless one has the goods to back it up. People who are great at something don't have to tell themselves they are. This is not because of any fake modesty, but because people of high self-esteem, however accomplished and competent, know that the more they know, the more there *is* to know. But they're confident that their minds have an infinite capacity to constantly expand. They have the ability to constantly grow, not only intellectually but spiritually, again for lack of a better word. And most importantly, their self-esteem comes from them. It's not something that can be bestowed on them by someone else. And the corollary is that, as I've already mentioned, it can't be taken away by someone else. This includes any random stranger yelling obscenities at them in the street or on the highway; anyone telling them they're stupid, ugly, untalented, or 'not enough.'"

"I understand what you're saying, Mildred. But didn't you say that some things *can* be judged objectively? A bad pianist, a bad painter? And aren't some people objectively ugly and some objectively beautiful?"

"Of course. That's why the saying 'beauty is in the eye of the beholder' is one of those classic bullshit phrases passed down from generation to generation. It's uttered so often that it's become an accepted 'truth.' I can't deny the fact that any random bikini model on this planet has an infinitely better body than I do, just like any Calvin Klein underwear model has a better body than *you* do. But that does not indicate a lack of self-esteem, because my self-esteem isn't contingent upon me *having* a bikini model's body. Do you remember what you told me when I asked you if it bothers you that you could never be as good a basketball player as Michael Jordan or as good a tennis player as Novak Djokovic?"

"Yeah. I said I didn't care, because those aren't my priorities."

"Precisely. And having a bikini-model body is not one of mine. But—and I'm not saying this to brag in any way, but just stating a simple truth—there's no bikini model on Earth that my husband would rather make love to than me. When Jim looks at me—fat, physically unattractive, dumpy old me—he's merely seeing the outer surface of the woman whose mind, sense of humor, and values he admires. What he sees on the surface is merely the outer wrapping of the gifts one finds when they rip off the wrapping paper.

"And do you know what, George? Jim is gorgeous, and I'm not just saying this as his proud wife. Women hit on him all the time. And that's fine with me, just as long as it's 'look, but don't touch.' And that *I* get to go home with him. But if he *weren't* physically attractive, I'd still love making love with him as much as he loves making love with me, because he means far more to me than just his great looks...even though he can't beat me in a philosophical debate." Mildred laughed.

"But you still haven't defined self-esteem," said George.

"Self-esteem is having a basic love for yourself. It doesn't mean we love everything we do on a daily basis. But we believe in our value, and we believe in our efficacy. If we don't love something about ourself, we change it if we can. If it's something that can't be changed, like our height, we accept it as a part of reality. And we don't base our self-esteem on what others think of us or think should be improved about us."

"Wait a minute. Shouldn't a young artist feel over the moon if a famous expert in their field tells them they're wonderful and highly gifted?"

"Of course. Being complimented, especially by a highly skilled person in our field we respect, feels so good. It also acts as inspiration to hone our skills and get better at whatever it is we aspire to. Part of this is to validate the opinion of the 'expert.' But it doesn't mean we should rest on our laurels. Always striving for improvement in things that are important to us, as well as accepting constructive criticism from people with more knowledge and skill than us, is essential for growth. We all need *constructive* criticism, especially gifted young children, and I emphasize the word *constructive*. That's what having a teacher is all about.

"In almost every avocation, there's almost always room for growth and improvement. But there's a difference between criticizing an act, result, or performance, and labeling a person based on a particular outcome. A young, impressionable student can be irreparably harmed if they're told they're stupid, or that they have no talent and will never make it in whatever it is they're passionate about. The student then feels like there's no reason to strive, because they've already been told that no matter what they do, their goal is impossible.

"Of course, one should always consider the source. Is this 'expert' labeling this youngster because they're jealous? They recognize this child's potential, but consider him or her to be a threat to their *own* self-esteem, because they consider *themselves* to be inadequate. By

thwarting the aspirations of an impressionable youngster, they effectively eliminate the competition. If the
youngster were not thwarted, and went on to become
'better' than the 'expert,' it would deliver an even greater
blow to their self-esteem.

"Then you have situations where a highly skilled
and talented 'expert' negatively labels a youngster solely out of maliciousness. It gives them a lot of 'power,'
or at least how they define it. But history is strewn
with examples of 'experts' telling writers, musicians,
dancers, painters, athletes, actors, or what have you,
that they shouldn't give up their day jobs because they
would never make it…and the aforementioned going
on to achieve dazzling success. As Aristotle famous-
ly said, 'There is only one way to avoid criticism: do
nothing, say nothing, and be nothing.'

"And speaking of criticism, I respect *any* artist
more than any critic. Even if a performer gives an objectively poor performance, at least they're confront-
ing risk; at least they're striving; at least they're putting
themselves out there, putting themselves on the line.
Remember, George, 'There is no success unless the
possibility of failure exists.' That's Robert Schuller. Or
bear in mind one of my favorite quotes of all time, by
Jean Sibelius: 'No statue was ever erected for a critic.'

"Unfortunately, a youngster often hasn't grasped the motivations of those who would want to discourage them. Tragically, many abandoned their dreams because of the words of an 'expert,' and never lived to find out that had they not given up their pursuit, they would've thrived."

"So how do you deal with malicious criticism, Mildred?"

"One way is to become your own most severe critic. That way, no one could ever evaluate you more severely than you do yourself. Another way is to develop an emotional 'firewall,' like what I mentioned previously in regard to the Poker Queen. In other words, you develop enough self-esteem so that nothing anyone says to you can affect you. Now, am I saying that a person of high self-esteem can't have their feelings hurt? No. But there's a difference between being emotionally affected by what others say and having enough confidence and feelings of self-worth so that we're not immobilized by the words of another, especially a random stranger.

"One time, I read a really malicious review of a book I loved. The critic happened to be a 'writer' herself, and I use that term in quotes. Just out of curiosity, I read one of *her* books, and the writing was so poor, with such a multitude of appalling grammatical errors, that it was actually horrifying that someone would present something like that to the public…and want to get paid for it, no less. I didn't know whether to laugh or cry. A critic like that criticizing another writer is like the Hunchback of Notre Dame calling Miss Universe ugly!

"I wouldn't make a good critic, George, because I always felt that if I couldn't do better than the one I was criticizing, I shouldn't be criticizing them. And if I *could* do better, I should be up on the stage or composing my own music, and not have all this extra time to sit around criticizing someone else.

"I once had a male patient who was forty and had never been married or in a relationship. Whenever he met a woman on a date, the inevitable question of why would always come up. When this man said he didn't know, the woman then eliminated him from contention, because she thought something must be wrong with him. One time, a divorced woman he met on a date made a really rude remark to him, but at least he had what I considered the perfect comeback this time: 'You failed at marriage, and yet you pass judgment on me?!'

"All of this has me thinking of Tony, too. Tony's a dear friend and a wonderful person, but he does have a violent temper, and any injustices he hears about enrage him. We've had a lot of discussions about this. He told me that anyone cursing him or giving him the finger when he's driving, for example, makes him want to kill the other person. But then he had a revelation. He told himself—and Jim and I feel the same way— that unless he lived on a desert island, he was always going to come across rude people, people who didn't like him, and people who would curse him.

"Tony realized that by acting out on his rage, he could get himself killed or sent to prison for the rest of his life. Is it really worth it to throw your life away over what a random piece of shit in the street says to you? So, with a lot of reflection, he developed his own firewall regarding these situations. A person can say anything they want about him and call him any obscenity in the book. He's able to do a pretty good job of letting that stuff bounce right off him. The words are nothing but sounds. But—and this is a huge *but*—the moment you lay a hand on him, you're going to get hurt.

"High self-esteem doesn't mean we're totally evolved. Quite the contrary. This is how great minds and talents evolve and get even greater. Recognizing that we're not at the level we want to be is not indicative of weakness; it's indicative of wisdom. And the more we strive and learn, the more we realize there *is* to learn. But the learning and striving alone increases our knowledge, our level of understanding, and our efficacy. In other words, when we conquer one goal, we realize that we have the *ability* to conquer other goals."

"Sometimes people work extremely hard and do not achieve their goals," said George.

"That's often because they view their goals as what they think they *should* be. Do you know who David Ferrer is?"

"The former professional tennis player?"

"That's right. At one point, he was the number three ranked player in the world. I think you'd agree that nobody could be the third ranked player in the world if they weren't a fantastic player. But in seventeen professional matches with Federer, he never won."

"I'm sure that really ate at him."

"Undoubtedly. Even though he was better than over 99.9 percent of professional tennis players."

"But when you're at that level, you don't compare yourself to country club instructors. You compare yourself to the best in the world, because that's what you're striving to be."

"True," Mildred agreed. "But should the fact that he never beat Federer make him consider himself a failure? Only one player can win a match. And some players who *have* beaten Federer have never won a Grand Slam singles title."

"So, what *does* someone do when they don't reach their ultimate goals in the things they consider very important to them? The things they use to define themselves?"

"They establish things they can take away from the experiences. For example, in those seventeen matches that Ferrer lost to Federer, he won six sets. This is significant, because a set isn't just a game. It's a group of games. And no player can take a set from a world-class player, especially an all-time great, without being pretty damn good themselves. And one of the sets that Ferrer won was 6-1, almost a blowout. And some of the players that Ferrer beat have beaten Federer."

"But if you were Ferrer's sports psychologist or coach, what would you have told him in reference to dealing with that pretty serious monkey on his back of never having beaten Federer?"

"I would've had him make sure he was following every conceivable protocol regarding fitness, preparation, working on weaknesses, diet, sleep, etc. I'd make sure he was watching films of Federer playing other opponents in addition to himself and analyzing any possible tendency that could give him an edge. When playing Federer, I'd emphasize and analyze the element of risk versus reward, and develop a strategy.

"But ultimately, I'd stress that it was even more important that he play the ball rather than a specific opponent. And that even if he did lose, because of the enormous challenge he faced and his enormous preparation, if it nonetheless lifted his game and made him a better player, that was still a positive thing. He should be in competition with *himself* more than any individual opponent. Do you think the second-richest billionaire in the world is upset because he's not number one on the Forbes list?

"And by the way, there've been times when an unheralded player has beaten Federer. Same with Nadal, Djokovic, and all the greats. In those cases, had I been the coach of one of those players, I would've jumped on this during their training. Obviously, even the greatest of the great can have an off day. They might've already played three back-to-back five-setters, be injured, not feeling well, going through personal problems, etc.

"But be that as it may, nobody can win a match against Federer or the rest if they're not enormously talented and have great potential. A player who's beaten one of these masters already has a huge psychological advantage the next time he plays one of them. He now knows it's possible to beat them, and that if he can play at his absolute best, it's entirely realistic that he can win again, especially if the other player has another off day.

"And speaking of tennis, do you know who Stan Wawrinka is?"

"Of course, Mildred."

"Well, before I even knew who he was, I would always see his funny-sounding name, along with the same other names, pop up when I'd go online to check the results of various tournaments. It saddened me that almost all of those obviously fantastic players would never bust through and achieve something truly remarkable, like winning a Grand Slam singles tournament.

"But anyway, Wawrinka intrigued me, and it made me wonder if a player like him, who lived in the shadow of his celebrated Swiss compatriot, Roger Federer, could ever break through if he had the right coach and devoted every waking hour to training, fitness, proper diet, etc. And then, he did. In 2014, he beat Rafael Nadal in the finals of the Australian

Open. It was the first time since 1993 that a player had beaten the number-one and number-two seeds in the same Grand Slam singles tournament (he had beaten Novak Djokovic in the quarterfinals). It was also the first time he had beaten Nadal in thirteen attempts. In the previous twelve matches, he had never even won a single set. He achieved this at the age of twenty-eight, which is considered 'old' to win a major. On this occasion, it was Wawrinka's first appearance in the finals of a major; it was Nadal's nineteenth.

"The next year, 2015, he defeated Novak Djokovic in the finals to win the French Open, and in 2016, he again defeated Djokovic in the finals to win the US Open.

"Referring to Federer, Nadal, and Djokovic, he has said he's not as good as those guys. In terms of consistency and career achievements, maybe he's right. But if I had been his coach or sports psychologist, I would *never* encourage him to make such a statement. In all three Grand Slam singles tournaments that he won, he beat the number one player in the world on three of tennis's biggest world stages. And on those occasions, it could have been argued that he was the best in the world.

"Now, George, what I said regarding Wawrinka does not just apply to him and to tennis. It applies to anyone and any endeavor. The only exception I would make is when someone is negatively assessing their ability in something of little importance to them. For example, I will gladly admit that I'm a lousy cook, golf player, etc., because these things mean nothing to me, and I don't *care* that I'm no good at them. And I know you feel the same way about things that hold little importance to *you*. But when we get to things that *do*, we should *never* negatively label ourself, especially in comparison to another person. Because if *you* don't think you're a great pianist, for example, why should others believe otherwise? Shouldn't your own assessment be construed as the most accurate? In addition, we tend to limit ourselves to the labels we place on ourselves. We tend to live up to our own assessments and expectations, just like self-fulfilling prophecies often come true.

"Vladimir Ashkenazy is a truly great pianist. One of the pieces he recorded was Beethoven's Concerto No. 5 (*Emperor*). He was also the conductor when Evgeny Kissin recorded this. He said that Kissin played this concerto much better than he ever did. I would have never believed this, but who better to believe than Ashkenazy himself? When you make a definitive statement such as this, it in essence becomes *fact*. After a statement like this, why would anyone choose to buy the CD of Ashkenazy playing the *Emperor* rather than Kissin's version?

"In team sports, it's obviously more difficult to assess individual success. In a professional basketball game, when there are five players from one team on the court at one time, a couple of players having a poor game can be bailed out by one or two players having a fantastic game, and that team could still win. But with an individual sport like tennis, boxing, mixed martial arts and others, you're on your own, so you can't rely on another player to bail you out." She leaned back in her chair. "Now, George, tell me about what *you* want to be great at."

"I want to be a great pianist and musician."

"Do you think you are?"

"Not even close."

"So your self-esteem is suffering, because you feel like you can't measure up to the top people in your field?'

"That's right."

"It's interesting you brought up music, and specifically piano playing. Because here's something that *can't* be judged like a tennis match, basketball game or 50-yard dash, where there's a clear-cut winner and clear-cut losers."

"But didn't you mention a kid banging out 'Chopsticks' in comparison to Vladimir Horowitz playing a Chopin mazurka? Wouldn't it be reasonable to assert that Horowitz is the better pianist?"

"Of course. Because the difference in the skill level is so great that an objective assertion in this case would be entirely appropriate. I'm talking about pianists who are already highly skilled. When you're at this level, especially when you're referring to art, there can be no objective answer unless you're referring to specific things. Take Artur Schnabel and Simon Barere. What's the prevailing thought when these pianists are mentioned?"

"Well, Schnabel only played pieces he considered better than could be played. He specialized in Mozart, Beethoven, and Schubert. He wasn't concerned with pleasing his audiences. His only concern was to do justice to the composer. He's known for being technically sloppy and playing many wrong notes. But note-perfect virtuosity was never his *raison d'etre*. He was concerned with structure, architecture, and wrestling with the musical and emotional meanings of the works he performed.

"Barere was a fantastic technician who played accurately and lightning-fast. He was the kind of pianist who pleased the laymen in the audience because of the sheer visceral excitement he generated. But when great interpreters are mentioned, he's never included."

"So, who was the better musician?" asked Mildred. "It can't be answered, because it's an apples and oranges question. We have this concert pianist who performs at our home frequently. He's absolutely marvelous, and my guests always shower him with praise. But privately, he's lamented to me that he's so unhappy with how long it takes him to memorize a piece. The final result is always wonderful, but the process is sheer hell. But no one in the audience knows this. They're just hearing the final product, which is flawless.

"Another of the concert pianists who performs for us has told me he'd give ten years of his life to be able to play with the fluency and polish the other pianist displays. But this pianist happens to be able to memorize virtually overnight. And as a sight reader, he's unbelievable. Someone can place a difficult piece in front of him that he never saw before, and he can play it as if he'd been practicing it for months. The first pianist, in addition to complaining about how long it takes him to memorize a piece, also laments that he's always been a lousy sight reader. So, which one of these two is more talented?"

"Mildred, everything you say makes a lot of sense, but isn't our opinion about ourselves and our abilities in various endeavors based on comparison? If there were no 'standard,' there'd be no means for evaluation. If everyone in the world were obese, then being obese would not be called that, but would be the norm."

"But this isn't how the world is. You're speaking in hypotheticals."

"Come on, Mildred. As a philosopher, I'd think you of all people should recognize that hypotheticals are necessary for critical evaluation, and as a basis for evaluating the legitimacy of our premises. Have you not written about lifeboat scenarios, where only a certain amount of people could fit in a lifeboat? How do you decide who gets saved and who perishes? Of course, these situations don't come up often, but the answers to these questions provide clues to our critical thinking and judgments, as well as to our moral fiber."

"You're right, George, they do. But this stuff is a whole other issue, a whole other discussion. And of course, it's important and legitimate. But the fact is, we live in a world where there are fat people, skinny people, tall people, short people, beautiful people, ugly people, people with subaverage intelligence, people with above-average intelligence, good people, bad people, talented people, untalented people...the list goes on and on. The question is, how do you evaluate and process all of this? How do you make sense of this so that you develop your own standard as to how you'll live your life, how you'll think, what opinion you'll hold about yourself, no matter what goes on around you?

"Whether someone's in a mansion or a concentration camp, the circumstances you've been placed in—especially those beyond your control—don't define you as a person. Your *reaction* to these situations and how you *handle* them do. If self-esteem is your irreducible primary, then it's not contingent on the whims or opinions of other people, nor on the circumstances that come up. And to make a comparison to something like the crime epidemic currently plaguing our cities, we must also consider our inalienable right to sovereignty and safety as a given...regardless of the circumstances."

A week later, George met with Mildred again. "Mildred, some people claim that if there were no

God, there could be no objective protocol for judging 'good and bad.'"

"This is bullshit. It sounds like something Irwin would say."

"Irwin?"

"Irwin Markov, or 'Professor' Markov, as he likes to be called. The only similarity between us are the first four letters of our last names. He has a PhD in philosophy and theology, is a devout Catholic, has won every award in his fields, and has acolytes all over the world. Because he speaks so eloquently, and tells everyone what they want to hear, everyone always laps up everything he says.

"He thinks that since atheists don't believe in God, they're unable to objectively determine good and bad. Religionists then win by default. When people of his ilk are then asked about atheists who always try to treat others the way they like to be treated, they're similarly dismissed. Meanwhile, if you ask them about atrocities committed in the name of religion, like certain African tribes who mutilate young girls' genitals (to name just one egregious example), they say that what appear to be evil acts to most people are not actually evil, because the people doing them thought they were doing the right thing."

"But if a person doesn't think they're doing wrong, wouldn't they be considered morally superior to the person who commits the same act but *intends* to cause harm or pain? That doesn't add up. What about a totally 'good' person who kills someone by accident? The outcome is the same as if a bad person killed an innocent person deliberately. But the bad person often goes to jail, while the good person remains unpunished."

"Unpunished?"

"Yeah. He didn't go to jail."

"Do you think sending someone to jail is the only way the person can be punished?"

"You know what I mean. He didn't pay for what he did."

"Pay who? Society? What about the self-inflicted pain that a good person is feeling for causing harm to a good, innocent person? If I accidentally hurt an innocent person, I'd have trouble living with my conscience."

"So would I. But determining motivation and who's sorry or not isn't always easy."

"Granted. It's *not* always easy, and that brings up other issues. But we were discussing how to determine the difference between good and evil when we objectively know the perpetrator's intent."

"Well, how *could* you determine it if there were no God?"

"By establishing basic premises and proceeding from there."

"Come on, Mildred. What if people have different premises? We've all heard that people can have different realities."

"That is a totally contradictory statement."

"What's your definition of reality?"

"Reality is what *is*. It doesn't care what your *perception* of reality is. I am a woman by definition. If someone perceived me to be a man, would that make it true?"

"Well, let's get back to how to determine the difference between good and evil. Most people say that in life, not everything is black or white. There are grey areas sometimes."

"Well, those people are right some of the time, and not right some of the time."

"What do you mean by *that*?"

"If someone makes a statement that mustard is better than ketchup on hot dogs, then I would grant that this is a grey area. Neither choice is 'right' or 'wrong,' because different people have different taste buds and therefore different preferences. And in things such as this, I wouldn't *want* an objective answer anyway. I like the idea that all people are different, like different things, have different interests, and have different opinions on issues. That's what makes life interesting. I think if everyone were clones, it'd make life rather boring.

"But in the realm of determining good and evil, there are no grey areas when motivation has been established. This does *not* mean that people who commit evil acts, but think they're doing 'right,' shouldn't be stopped or punished, such as the tribes we were discussing before who think it's okay to mutilate the genitals of young girls."

"Okay, I'd agree with you that that kind of behavior should be stopped. But if they think they're doing good, why would you call them evil?"

"Well, I wouldn't consider them to be as evil as a tribe who committed these acts solely for purposes of recreation or pleasure. But nevertheless, any good or moral person would want these acts stopped, regardless of the motivation of the perpetrators. They should be stopped and punished because they're causing pain and suffering. If what they're doing is so 'righteous,' why don't they sacrifice *themselves*?

"Secondly, if you lock up or kill a person intent on hurting an innocent person, you prevent them from hurting or killing others. Yes, I would place the people who legitimately thought what they were doing was 'right' on a slightly higher moral plane than the people who deliberately wanted to cause pain and suffering for their own enjoyment. But regardless of the motivation, the outcome would be the same.

"Bernie Madoff was an evil man, even though he'd never hit an old woman on the street over the head with a baseball bat or rape her. Just because the pain and destruction he caused was of a different nature, would you not agree he was every bit as evil as the rapist?

"When we talk about something like the mutilators of young girls' genitals, it doesn't matter what rung on the ladder of evil they're standing. Regardless of their specific motivation, they're committing unambiguously evil acts, and should be stopped by whatever means necessary. And for the Markovs of the world who would keep bringing up the argument of motivation, it would be *his* responsibility to prove that the gods wanted them to commit such acts. What about religions that completely disagree with the practice of genital mutilation, but commit *other* atrocities? Are these religions not totally convinced of the rectitude of *their* actions?

"In relation to good and evil, there *are* no grey areas, George. De facto evil is not subject to your opinion of what it is. Some things *are* black and white. Like I told you, even with the limitations inherent in us being human and mere 'mortals,' this doesn't mean that basic premises regarding decency can't be established. I hope you're not saying that since different people believe different things, there are alternate realities. There is no such thing, and as I've already told you, this statement is a contradiction in terms. Just because we don't know all the answers doesn't mean that there *are* no answers. There *is* an explanation as to the origin of the universe. There *is* an answer as to whether or not God exists, and there *is* an answer as to whether or not certain events happened or didn't happen.

"But different religions believe diametrically different things. Obviously, all cannot be right. Only one—at most—can be right as to whether something happened or not, or whether something exists or not. This is a basic law of logic. Something cannot exist and not exist at the same time. Something could have either happened or not have happened. Period."

"So, what's the answer, Mildred?"

"I don't know all the answers, George. But until I do—either through the irrefutable evidence from my senses or from irrefutable scientific evidence—I will never pretend, as all religious people do, to know what cannot be known, or at least at this time. An intelligent person always discovers that the more someone knows, the more there *is* to know."

"Yeah, but what about the people who say that you can't prove there is no God?"

"First of all, I'd never make such a definitive statement, that there is no God. I might not believe it, but I'll never say there's no chance of it. I will say that there's no way of logically determining whether or not there is one, and therefore I will not invent one to suit my purposes. I will not invent one because I want the comfort of thinking that some omniscient, omnibenevolent heavenly father up there is looking out for me. I will not invent one because it is the 'right' thing to do. And I certainly will not invent one because everyone else believes in one.

"But if having this belief serves the purpose of bringing joy, comfort, and hope to someone, I'm all for having this person believe whatever they want...however misguided I might feel them to be." She chuckled. "If they live their life guided by what they consider to be the highest moral principles, then it's none of my business to try to convince them otherwise. Similarly, I'd never ask them to prove to me that there was a tooth fairy. I do happen to believe in Santa Claus, however, because I've actually seen him...on Fifth Avenue, in Macy's, Nordstrom, and all the other department stores during the holidays. But as for being able to prove there's no God...never let yourself be goaded into falling for that trap, George. Asking someone to prove a negative is a ploy that's been used throughout history. It's like the word game that people employ to 'prove' that God can't do everything. Chaim Potok cited this in one of his novels.

"They'll ask, 'If God can do everything, does that mean He can make a rock so heavy that even He couldn't lift it?' People are then supposed to answer that of course, He could. If He couldn't, then that would mean He couldn't do everything. And then they're told that if God could lift the rock, then that also means he can't do everything, because he couldn't create a rock too heavy for Him to pick up. And many people fall for this example of a logical impossibility. It's just like when people say, 'Heads, I win; tails, you lose.'"

George was dying to explore other issues with Mildred, and asked if there were a time next week when he could continue speaking with her. "Of course," she replied. "Would Wednesday evening be convenient?"

"Sure."

"And by the way, I've actually been challenged to a debate by Markov. The topic is 'prison reform,' and will be held on the thirteenth in Alden Hall."

"I'd love to go, Mildred."

CHAPTER FOUR

Alden Hall was filled to capacity. Professor Markov made sure all his students came, and urged them to invite all their family and friends. His own cheering section represented one of his perceived advantages over Mildred. The debate was to be a discussion format. Time limits and biased moderators asking questions were to be considered a hindrance. A moderator, the one who introduced them, was present, but would only intervene in the case of a shouting match or both parties talking over one another.

"Good evening, Doctor Markowitz," Markov began.

"Good evening, Professor Markov."

"Ladies and gentlemen," said Professor Markov, "it seems that Doctor Markowitz and I have quite pronounced differences in our views regarding morality, crime, and the criminal justice system. A woman of your stature," he said, while addressing Doctor Markowitz, "should surely concede that the issue of crime and punishment is a much more complex issue than simply locking up the so-called bad guys."

"What's wrong, professor, in punishing people who do bad things?"

"Your question, doctor, is obviously too simplistic. It doesn't take into account a person's upbringing, socio-economic status, whether or not the person is homeless or mentally ill, and a whole host of other issues."

"Okay, professor, let's say someone's on a subway platform going to work, and as the train is approaching the station, he's suddenly pushed onto the tracks and killed. Should the perpetrator not be punished?"

"Doctor, before continuing this discussion, I think we should establish what kind of crimes we're addressing. Surely, there are differences between jaywalking, embezzlement, armed robbery, rape, drunk driving, and murder."

"Obviously, professor, there are differences in the severity of crimes. People don't go to jail for jaywalking or parking violations. For the latter, they get a ticket and pay a fine. Moving up the hierarchy, I'm also not suggesting that someone caught shoplifting or committing a so-called 'white collar crime' should receive the same punishment as the person who sodomizes and kills a little girl. A person who shoplifts or a politician caught taking a bribe can make financial restitution. But a murderer can never bring the person they killed back, and a rapist can never undue the catastrophic harm and life-altering scars they inflict on their victims."

"That is true, doctor. But I'm not so sure these kinds of crimes deserve a 'lock 'em up and throw away the key' solution."

"Well, since you don't feel, professor, that violent crimes do not merit at *least* a 'lock 'em up and throw away the key' solution, why don't we confine our discussion to the issue of violent crime?"

"Agreed. We'll focus on so-called 'violent' crime."

"So-called?"

"Well, as you mentioned, doctor, a parking ticket is a more 'minor' offense than a rape or homicide. Wouldn't you agree that there are similarly different levels of violent crime, as you call it? Someone convicted of drunk driving shouldn't be considered a violent criminal, nor receive the same punishment that a rapist or murderer should, because their intention wasn't to cause harm."

"But if being drunk and getting behind the wheel of a car—even though we are inundated with signs on the roads and commercials in the media stating over and over again that one should not drink and drive—resulted in the death of an entire family, should the driver not be severely punished?"

"Not necessarily."

"Not necessarily?!"

"What if the drunk driver gets to their destination *without* getting into an accident? Should they receive the same punishment as the driver who ends up in the accident that resulted in the death of the family?"

"I didn't say they should receive the same punishment. In this case, since the outcome was vastly different than the other scenario, I wouldn't mete out the same punishment as the driver who killed the family. But I would severely punish them nonetheless. It was only because of 'luck,' 'fate,' or whatever you want to call it, that the scenario didn't turn out the same. But to suggest that the drunk driver who killed the family shouldn't be severely punished simply *because* had the other car not been there, he wouldn't have harmed anyone, is absurd."

"Then I take it, doctor, you're saying that intent to cause harm shouldn't be taken into account when deciding what punishment to mete out."

"Intention does play a role. Certainly, someone who accidentally causes harm or death is not as 'morally' culpable as the one who deliberately causes the equivalent harm or death. But in the case of the drunk driver who killed the family but didn't intend to, the outcome is the same as if someone deliberately killed them. Let's imagine the scenario of an airline pilot encountering a violent storm. The plane ends up crashing and the pilot survives, but some of the passengers are killed. The pilot wasn't necessarily 'negligent.' In fact, he was considered a competent pilot. But his experience was not yet at the level that could pull him through in an emergency situation such as above. Had Sully Sullenberger been the pilot on this occasion, there would've been no casualties. Should this pilot be severely punished?"

"No, doctor. Not only did he not intend for there to be casualties, but he was not negligent. He was only guilty of not possessing the necessary advanced skill, poise, and experience that could've averted the result. Captain Sullenberger, as you stated, could've gotten everyone out of the situation unharmed. But a pilot with Sullenberger's skill, experience, and poise under extreme pressure is rare."

"Precisely. But in this case, professor, the pilot wasn't negligent, as you correctly indicated, but the drunk driver was. That's the big difference. I agree that the drunk driver who didn't intend to kill is less morally culpable than the drunk driver who did. But in this case, it didn't make any difference to the family that perished. Either way, they're just as dead."

"Okay, doctor, let's confine our discussion to deliberate violent crime."

"Fine. Let's do so."

"Good. I'm sure your contention is that two perpetrators of the same type of violent crime should receive equivalent punishment. Would I be correct in assuming that this is your position?"

"Yes."

"So, I take that to mean that if a mentally ill homeless man pushes someone in front of an oncoming train in the subway, his crime is just as bad as if a non-mentally ill man did it."

"Okay, professor, let's imagine the following scenario: You're on the subway platform with your wife. A train is approaching the station. All of a sudden you see a man running toward your wife. You realize his intention; he's about to push her in front of the train. You're licensed to carry a gun, which you have on you. You have time to shoot the man, and if you do, he would not be able to push your wife in front of the train. Do you shoot him?"

"Of course I do."

"Why?"

"Isn't it obvious, doctor? Because my wife's life is of far greater value to me than the life of someone who would needlessly take it from her."

"Bravo, professor. I couldn't have said it better myself."

"But if the person were mentally ill, schizophrenic, heard voices telling him to do it, etc., he wouldn't have been as culpable as someone who did this solely out of maliciousness or hate."

"Professor, how would you characterize the mental state of someone who would push an innocent person onto the tracks, just because he had a lot of hate in his heart?"

"Ah, doctor, but where does this hate come from?"

"Please don't evade my question, professor. We're not discussing the origins of his hate. We're discussing the 'now,' the present. One's upbringing, socio-economic situation, and parents can certainly be strong contributing factors to the genesis of his political views, sense of life, and hate. But we're not discussing the causes. That's a different discussion. As I said, we're discussing the present. An alcoholic is an alcoholic because they're addicted to alcohol; a drug addict is addicted to drugs regardless of whether or not their parents were drug addicts and taught them to shoot up before they realized how deadly drugs are."

"But didn't you concede earlier, doctor, that a person who intends to commit a bad act is more culpable than someone who commits the same act but didn't intend to?"

"So, assuming this is true, professor, why would you have shot the guy who was going to push your wife in front of the train?"

"Because I didn't have *time* to learn about his situation."

"Thank you, professor, for making my point."

"But are you not saying that a mentally ill person is less responsible for their actions than someone who knows exactly what they're doing?"

"Need I remind you, professor, about the drunk driver who kills a family but doesn't intend to, and the angry driver who kills a family because of road rage? In both cases, the victims are just as dead."

"Doctor, not everything in life is just cold, hard logic. Your arguments sound fancy on the surface, but you constantly ignore the human element. Not everything in life is black-and-white. There are grey areas as well. Everyone has different contexts and upbringings, and there are myriad reasons why people do the things they do or learn to do the things they do. You of all people should know that."

"Professor, is Putin an evil man?"

"There you go again, asking me to give a black-and-white assessment of someone."

"Professor, if someone who didn't know her asked you to describe your wife, what would you tell them?"

"I'd say she was the most beautiful, loving, caring, selfless, and understanding person I've ever met." In his eagerness to describe his wife and soulmate, the professor did not realize the trap he had fallen into until he finished his statement and heard giggling from the audience.

"Professor," said Mildred, "I don't know your wife, but I'm certain she possesses all the qualities you just spelled out. I'm also certain that if I met her, I'd come to the same conclusion. Now, you and I have never met Putin. But as a psychologist, and most importantly as a human being, let me save you the trouble. Putin is a totally and unambiguously monstrously evil man. You had mentioned that if someone were mentally ill, they're not to be considered as responsible for committing crimes as someone who knows what they're doing. Notwithstanding the fact that Putin knows ex-

actly what he's doing, it's been argued that he's a sociopath, because part of the definition is someone with
no compassion. And *being* a sociopath is considered
to be a mental illness…something *you* deem to be a
mitigating factor in determining culpability. Blowing
up innocent men, women, children and babies, and
specifically targeting places such as schools and hos-
pitals, is the equivalent of drinking a glass of water to
him. An innocent person's suffering, and the agony of
a man seeing his wife and children murdered right in
front of his eyes, holds zero significance to him.

"But, especially in the case of someone like Putin, I
consider the word *sociopath* to be, if not a justification,
a somehow clinical explanation as to how anyone could
commit such unspeakable atrocities. When I think of
Putin, however, the word *sociopath* doesn't come to
mind…only pure evil. Yet he wears Brioni suits; he'll
shake the hand of the leader of another country, and
they'll be offered cocktails and dinner. I once saw a
seventeen-year-old blind girl interview him on You-
Tube. Her goal was to be a journalist and interview
famous people. Putin agreed to be interviewed by her.
His tenderness with this girl was actually touching. It
gave me a lot of food for contemplation.

"But then I remembered that I've seen other evil people—famous and not famous—who could actually be pleasant and soft-spoken. Amidst their bestiality, sometimes snippets of humanity could occasionally surface. Often, this seeming contradiction between what one's true nature was and what they *appeared* to be was merely a mask. Jeffrey Dahmer's parents loved him. Have you seen the interviews with him on YouTube? He was actually soft-spoken, articulate, and personable, not some wild-eyed, crazed lunatic like Charles Manson, for example. He readily admitted that he definitely deserved the death penalty. And when he was asked what he thought when one of his victim's relatives was screaming obscenities at him in court, he said, 'I don't blame her one bit. I would have done the same thing.'

"Hitler was reputed to have been soft-spoken and even polite in private. Convicted serial killer Richard Kuklinski, aka 'the Ice Man,' murdered someone who owed him 600 dollars. After he killed him, he took his 600 dollars back. But the guy had more than that in his wallet. He could've taken everything, especially since the guy would no longer be needing the extra cash. But he only took what he was owed.

"In everyday life, you see crazed maniacs screaming obscenities at you at stoplights. I've had drivers behind me who wanted to kill me because I was driving too slowly for them, even when I was driving above the speed limit. But I'm sure all of you have heard that some of the biggest con artists are the ones you least suspect. With serial killers or scammers, they can actually be very personable and likable when you first meet them. It's part of their ruse. That is what's made them so successful. Who would you be more likely to hand over your life savings to—a mean-spirited and abusive weirdo, or an immaculately dressed, polite, friendly, and personable guy? A wolf in sheep's clothing? I happen to have a patient who was hurt by an evil woman…a woman who could actually be pleasant and polite to his face."

"Doctor, all of those examples you just mentioned only lends credence to the argument I've always been a proponent of: there's good in all people."

"Quite the contrary, professor. Just because one might observe snippets of so-called civilized behavior or humanity does not negate that these are all *fundamentally* bad people. Nazis torturing a prisoner in a concentration camp were known to derive extreme pleasure the louder their victim's screams became. Some of them even got off sexually. Would you consider these monsters any less evil because they gave their mothers flowers on their birthday?

"But we've digressed, so let's get back to our discussion. Professor Markov has stated that one's upbringing and context have a lot to do with shaping their worldview and behavior. He also stated that sometimes a homeless or mentally ill person doesn't know what they're doing. Sometimes a person is schizophrenic and legitimately hears voices telling them what to do. All this is true. But the fact is, when Professor Markov's wife was about to be pushed in front of an oncoming train, his instincts were to save his wife's life. The other information didn't matter to him. And if it did, and if it had a bearing on the crime, it was irrelevant and there was no time to find out. Whatever the situation happened to be, his wife's life held precedence. This is how it should be, and I would've done the same thing."

"Yes, doctor, in these so-called emergency situations, one doesn't have time to process the particulars of a perpetrator's situation. I concede that one often has a split second to make a decision, and this decision will very often determine the outcome of the incident. But aside from emergency situations, would you not agree that a person's upbringing should be taken into account when determining what punishment they should receive? Some people come from broken homes; they could've been raised by a single parent; both parents could've been alcoholics or drug addicts; they could've been beaten or sexually abused; they could've been homeless; they could've been mentally ill."

"Yes, professor, the perpetrator could've been one or all of those things. But in the case of raping or killing an innocent person, the outcome would've been the same."

"So are you suggesting, doctor, that since the outcome might've been the same, the accountability on the part of the perpetrator should similarly be the same?"

"I'm not *suggesting* this, professor. I'm *stating* this. In the scenario we were discussing, were you or were you not happy that the person who was about to push your wife in front of the train was killed?"

"I'm not happy when anyone is killed, doctor."

"Oh really? What would've happened to your wife had the man not been shot dead?"

"You're trying to get me to state that I'm happy someone was killed, doctor. I'm not happy someone was killed. I will never be happy when someone is killed. Unlike you, I happen to believe in the sanctity of human life and the inherent good in all people. Who are you to judge someone's goodness? Only God can judge."

"You didn't answer my question, professor. What would've happened to your wife had the man not been shot dead?"

"Of course, she would've been killed under your scenario. But that doesn't mean I'd be happy if the man were killed. He was still a child of God, and for that reason, God loved him. And at one time, he had parents or family members who loved him. I was happy that my wife was saved."

"Professor, one of the laws of the universe is something that Ayn Rand wrote about: A equals A. It means that existence exists, that something either exists or it doesn't; something either is or it isn't; a person cannot be in more than one place at one time; one plus one can never equal three, no matter how much we might want it to. Someone cannot have their cake and eat it too. Your pious and self-righteous declarations will undoubtedly garner support from your acolytes in the

audience, because they sound so 'good' and 'ethical'…
especially since you inserted religion into the equation.
Well, I'll give you *my* assessment in one word: Bullshit.

"You shot your wife's attacker because your wife
represented a higher value to you than the scum who
would take her life. It didn't matter what this person's
context was. Had he been a career criminal, mentally
ill, or a priest in the Catholic Church who had mo-
lested many children, was all irrelevant. Let me ask
you something, professor. President Trump ordered
the hit of Qasem Soleimani, who was taken out when
a missile hit his car. It was a targeted assassination.
Should this not have been ordered?"

"No. We do not have the right to kill someone.
Only God does. If we do kill someone, then it's murder."

"Professor, it has been documented that Soleimani
was responsible for the deaths of many Americans. Do
you dispute this?"

"No. But that doesn't give us the right to kill him.
As I've stated, only God has that right."

"So, by killing him, this would constitute revenge?"

"That's right."

"And revenge, I take it, is something that is morally wrong."

"Yes, because two wrongs don't make a right."

"You're certainly up on all the well-known cliches, professor; I'll give you that. It's been written that at the time of his 'departure,' Soleimani was in the process of planning future attacks on innocent Americans. Do you doubt this was true?"

"Maybe it was."

"So given this information, I take it you'd still consider taking him out to be morally wrong."

"That's right. You can't punish someone for what he hasn't done."

"So once he does it, then you can punish him?"

"That's right. But we don't have a right to kill him."

"But let's say we didn't kill him, and by not doing so, this resulted in him ordering the killing of one hundred Americans."

"As I said, we can punish him afterwards. We can't assume someone will do something before they do it."

"Even if that person had a pattern of doing those things in the past, and even though we might have credible intelligence to indicate he'll do it again?"

"That's right. To kill a man because of what we *think* he might do constitutes premeditated murder."

"Okay, professor. Imagine you're the president. You're informed of intelligence indicating that another attack on innocent Americans is imminent. But you decide not to take Soleimani out because, as you said, we can't assume someone will do something until he does it. Soleimani then proceeds to kill one hundred Americans. You would not consider yourself to be in any way morally culpable?"

"As I've already stated, doctor, God created people, so only God has the right to take a life."

"With all due respect, professor, I would consider you to have a lot of blood on your hands. And by the way…can you tell me what the difference was between the man on the subway you shot and Soleimani?"

"The man on the subway was *about* to push my wife to her death. This wasn't revenge. It was a preventative act."

"And the killing of Soleimani was not?"

"No. Because he didn't do it yet."

"Neither did the man on the subway kill your wife before you shot him."

"The fact that the guy was going to push my wife was imminent."

"So, because of the fact that Soleimani would've had many more Americans killed but not instantaneously means we shouldn't have taken preventative measures? In regard to killing Soleimani, I assert that the *fact* that he would've ordered the killing of many more Americans had he *not* been killed is every bit as credible as the fact that your wife would've been killed had you not killed her attacker. The same situations have occurred regarding criminals who have broken into bodegas and homes. Often, even after they've taken the money and jewelry, they kill the occupants anyway.

And by the way, professor, regarding all the criminals who came from broken homes, were raised by a single parent, or parents who were alcoholics, drug addicts, etc., have you considered the fact that many people who came from these environments went on to become wonderful, law-abiding citizens who accomplished amazing things?"

"But this isn't the norm."

"How do you know? Have you taken statistics?"

"You can't take statistics with these kinds of things. I know from observation."

"Yet you're saying that the severity of the punishment for a criminal should be mitigated based on the things I mentioned above regarding his upbringing."

"They should be taken into account."

"How would you quantify it? Different things affect people in different ways. What is preferable, professor, to have a child who's the product of divorce, or to be the child of an alcoholic? What's worse, to be the child of an alcoholic crack addict or the victim of sexual abuse?"

"There you go, doctor, talking technicalities..."

"You're the one who brought up a child's upbringing, professor. If you can't quantify the respective seriousness of a given situation opposed to another, you shouldn't be bringing this up."

"Doctor, I think you're well-aware that you can't quantify things like this. Every family has their own unique situation. And each one of those issues has varying degrees of severity. Taking a shower with your daughter might constitute sexual abuse, but is not as serious as incest."

"Thank you for making my point, professor. So why don't we only consider the severity of a deliberate crime, and mete out punishment accordingly?"

"I think I told you why."

"But if you can't even quantify the severity of life's challenges a child was brought up with, because each thing would be more or less severe depending upon the individual child, how could you then determine the appropriate punishment? And I'll remind you, professor, *you* were the one who brought up these extenuating circumstances to try to make excuses for the scum who would commit such atrocities." Markov remained silent. "And if you're including all the things you mentioned above, by that rationale you should also include his toilet training in your list of underlying criteria."

Now Mildred addressed the audience. "And let me remind the audience that Professor Markov has advocated that all White people should make reparations to all Black people, as well as embrace affirmative action because of the sins of our ancestors. Slavery, professor, was a horrific injustice. The concept of 'owning' another person you regard as inferior to you just because of the color of their skin is abhorrent. But even though slavery is no longer practiced in this country, and even though there are Black people who have achieved astounding success, he feels we still have a debt to pay. In that case, professor, Jews, whose ancestors burned in the ovens of Auschwitz solely because they were Jewish, should be offered similar reparations. What was worse, professor, slavery or the Holocaust?"

Professor Markov gave no reply. He just glared at Mildred.

"Yes, professor, I agree that one's upbringing *can* be a contributing factor as to how someone turns out. And yes, I'm a strong advocate of deterrence by way of raising a child properly and with good values. I'm also a strong advocate of education as well as therapy for children suffering from depression. But," and now Mildred started to raise her voice, "if someone rapes, sodomizes, or murders an innocent person, his upbringing is no longer my concern. I consider him to be an animal, i.e., subhuman, and should then be dealt with so severely that the possibility of him ever doing it again is eliminated." Professor Markov again offered no response.

"I think this is a good time to take our lunch break," said the moderator. "Why don't we all plan to convene back here at 2:00 p.m. to continue our discussion. Thank you, Professor Markov and Doctor Markowitz."

* * *

At 2:00 p.m., everyone was already seated back in Alden Hall. The moderator came out and addressed the audience. "I hope everyone had a good lunch. Now it's time to continue. Doctor? Professor?"

Mildred and Markov proceeded to take the stage. Professor Markov spoke first. "A lot has been said about the criminal justice system. Does it disproportionately negatively affect the poor, who can't afford legal representation? Are mentally ill people as accountable for their actions as people who know what they're doing? Does their upbringing play a role in their accountability? And what are the appropriate punishments?

"My assertion, doctor, is that we are all children of God, and that He and He alone should be the ultimate arbiter as to what punishment should be meted out to people who have done wrong. Sinners can be saved, and that's why God brought His son Jesus Christ down to Earth to die on the cross for our sins. He did this so we could all be saved. Because we are all sinners, doctor."

"It seems to me, professor, that if God were all-powerful, He could've created people without sin, and wouldn't have needed to send His son down here to cleanse people of their sins. And why would God ever choose to sacrifice a 'higher' being for the benefit of a 'lower' one?"

"Just by posing that question, doctor, you expose your ignorance. Whatever God chooses to do or not to do is not subject to your opinion or interpretation. It is just and right just by virtue of the fact that that is God's choosing. You don't question the motivations or reasons of a supreme being. I've heard you use the term 'irreducible primary' before. Well, that is precisely what this is."

"Even if certain things don't make sense to us?"

"That's right, doctor; even if certain things don't make sense to you. When you become God, then you can pass judgment."

"Alright, professor, I'll keep that in mind. But being that He's not someone we can talk to on the telephone to ask for guidance, we were going to discuss the implementation of an effective criminal justice system."

"Your lack of respect is appalling."

"Well, since God created me, professor, and since I'm an imperfect sinner just by virtue of the fact that I'm not God, but merely a product of His creation, I hope that such an omnibenevolent being will forgive me of my sins. Now, if you don't mind, professor, I'd like to focus on the issue of how to determine the appropriate punishment for violent crimes. You mentioned someone's upbringing as an excuse for why people sometimes do the things they do."

"As a *reason*, doctor, or at the very least, a contributing factor."

"Fine. That means that if we could implement a better educational system, have community outreach programs, make therapy more available in our inner cities, etc., it would definitely be a positive thing. I agree with you that if kids didn't come from broken homes, didn't have crackheads or alcoholics for parents, weren't victims of sexual abuse, didn't have to suffer the scourges of poverty, didn't develop mental illness, and didn't succumb to the peer pressure to join gangs, this would decrease the amount of violent crime."

"That's right; because just like cancer, diabetes, and heart disease, we'd be addressing the causes and not just the symptoms. If we address the root causes of problems and focus on prevention, we effectively nip the problems in the bud. Then you don't have to worry about treating the symptoms."

"I do agree with you, professor, that all of the above would be positive things which could probably reduce the incidence of violent crime. That being said, you never answered the questions I asked before the break. Again, I must remind you that we'd never be able to quantify the various contributing factors. In other words, what's worse, sexual abuse or having crackheads for parents? Also, different children will be more affected or less affected by different things. For one kid, the traumatization of sexual abuse would be worse than having crackheads for parents. In another case, the reverse might be true.

"And I'll remind you, professor, that some kids who came from wealthy families where there *was* no sexual abuse, alcohol, drugs, or what have you, have gone on to commit horrific crimes. And some kids who were the product of poverty, sexual abuse, alcohol, drugs, neglect, having only one parent - who happened to be a prostitute - did *not* go on to a life of crime, but became upstanding citizens who achieved great things.

"Getting back to the analogy I made about your wife about to get pushed in front of an oncoming train…when you shot the perpetrator before he could kill your wife, I'm sure his upbringing was irrelevant to you. Your wife's life was your *only* consideration…as it should have been."

"I had no *time* to make the assessment, doctor."

"Alright, professor. Your kids have been kidnapped, or you're being held at gunpoint in your home. Your kids' murders and your possible own aren't imminent. Perhaps you and your kids won't be murdered if the kidnappers get a specific amount of money. Maybe you're only being held as ransom, although you can't know the perpetrators' true motive. Would the perpetrators' 'upbringing' be any more relevant to you than that of the perpetrator who was about to push your wife in front of the train?"

"I'm saying that once we're safely out of the situation, and the perpetrators are now on trial, his upbringing should determine the extent of his culpability and punishment."

"Wonderful, professor. With that logic, all people raised in poverty, and living with alcohol, drugs, violence, sexual abuse, and gangs, would then know they could commit any crime they wished with impunity, because people like you would always exist to give them a 'get out of jail free' card. And while they're free, they can then join the mobs who ransack a store and rob them blind. All they have to concern themselves with is to make sure they steal under 1,000 dollars of merchandise."

"You, doctor, are an example of someone who talks so 'rationally,' talks so 'logically,' and speaks so articulately. But let me tell you something, doctor. For all your fancy rationality and declarations, you have no *heart*. That's the difference between you and me."

"Professor, if you're referring to the people who've committed such evil and horrific crimes, you're right, and I plead guilty. I don't give a shit about those people. My *heart* and my compassion lie with their victims."

"Alright, doctor, let's hear your solution to the crime epidemic."

"I never pretended to have a solution, professor. But what I *will* tell you is something that would act as a huge deterrent. Would it eliminate the problem? No. But would it substantially reduce it? *That* I could guarantee. We should mandate specific sentences for specific crimes. Obviously, the race and financial situation of the perpetrator should play no part in the sentence. Now, just to clarify things…as I mentioned, I don't consider shoplifting to be as serious a crime as rape, sodomy, or murder, so I wouldn't issue a life sentence to a shoplifter. For the purposes of this discussion, I'd like to just focus on violent crime."

"If you don't mind, doctor, I'd like to begin."

"Certainly."

"Ladies and gentlemen, once the good doctor begins, she'll undoubtedly inundate you with anecdotes of people who've been victims of violent crime. Her depictions will surely evoke sympathy, if not outrage in you. After all, no decent person wants there to be crime, and no decent person wants to see innocent people fall victim to crime. But what she'll conveniently avoid mentioning is that issuing a life sentence or otherwise harsh punishment to a person convicted of a crime results in the victimization of the perpetrator. Granted, we all want to make sure that person doesn't commit another crime. But by punishing the criminal, we render ourselves no different than the perpetrator. We're merely seeking revenge. And revenge, ladies and gentlemen, doesn't solve anything. It's merely a manifestation of our blood lust, a justification for 'getting even,' a goal that can't be achieved.

"The harsh incarceration of the perpetrator strips them of their humanity, and ignores the fact that everyone can atone for their sins. And this is precisely why God sent His only son to Earth to die on the cross for *us*. If *God* can forgive, surely we lesser mortals can. We've all heard heartwarming stories of criminals who found Jesus while in prison. They were still confined behind the walls of the prison, but they were saved. And their salvation inspired them to spread the

Word, in deeds as well as words. If they'd been let out into society, God knows how much more they could've achieved." With that, the audience gave the professor a rousing ovation, and he proceeded to smugly glance at Mildred with a smile and a nod to punctuate the affirmation of his victory.

"You know, professor, when I told some of my acquaintances about our upcoming friendly debate here, they expressed dismay that there were people who didn't examine issues in their totality. People will pass judgment based on personal bias or beliefs, and people will support or not support a particular agenda based on what political party they happen to identify themselves with. To be intellectually honest, I have to admit that I've occasionally succumbed to the temptation. But as people who call ourselves philosophers, I feel we must hold ourselves to a higher standard. Is it realistic that our personal biases and experiences would never play a role in our opinions and convictions? No. We're all emotional beings as well as intellectual ones. But if given a choice, professor, between making decisions and coming to conclusions based on emotion or on principles, the latter should take precedence. *Reason* should guide us, and should mandate that we analyze the entire implications of a given issue or dilemma.

"Let me ask you a question, professor. Let's imagine someone commits a horrific crime and is sentenced to life in prison. Now, let's say, just for argument's sake, that by some dispensation, after six months the person is now completely as well as verifiably 'rehabilitated.' There's no possibility they'll ever commit a similar crime again. Should they be set free?"

"Of course, they should, doctor. For what purpose should they be left in prison? What good would having them remain there serve? Couldn't they be a much more productive and valuable member of society if they were allowed to go free? Wouldn't their stay in prison have served its purpose, namely to rehabilitate them and then allow them to return to society as a productive member? To me this would be the ideal outcome of the true purpose of incarceration. To keep a person locked up after this goal is achieved constitutes nothing more than punishment. And punishment, doctor, is a form of revenge. It also keeps the person away from their family."

"Keeps them away from their family?! And the murderer who took the life of a little girl doesn't permanently keep *her* from her family, and her family from *her*? You really have a way with words, professor. But let me ask you just one small question. When you release this 'rehabilitated' person after six months, what do you then say to the parents and relatives of the little girl who was raped, sodomized, murdered, and dismembered? The perpetrator would've had a six-month sentence; the girl's loved ones have a *life* sentence. Do you think that kind of sentence is any better just because they're not behind bars?"

The professor suddenly found himself at a loss for words. He looked at the moderator, and his glance was a plea for help. "I think this is a good time for a coffee break," said the moderator. "Let's all return to our seats in ten minutes."

After ten minutes, the debate was resumed, and this time Mildred began first. "As I started to mention earlier, regarding horrific violent crimes, there should be mandates as to what the punishment should be, just as there are for DWI convictions. Now, in the latter, even though there are signs everywhere on the highways, commercials on TV, etc., warning about the dangers of drunk driving, as well as the consequences for doing so, people still drink and drive. And even after they're caught, they're still almost always given a second chance, even though their driving while intoxicated resulted in the death or injury of innocent people.

"The reason they're given a second chance is because most of the time, they had no malicious intent. They didn't think their drinking would affect them. Perhaps they drank and drove before and nothing happened. They rationalize that they're only driving a short distance, that driving was the only way they could get home, that they would drive more slowly, be more careful, or that they were the kind of person who could hold their liquor.

"But in the case I mentioned before the break of a rapist who sodomizes, murders, then dismembers a little girl, this is first of all almost always premeditated, as if a spontaneous act such as this wouldn't be horrific enough. It's depraved, cruel, and evil beyond human comprehension. It not only destroys the life of a beautiful little girl, as well as prevents her from one day giving birth to other beautiful children, but it permanently destroys the lives of her parents and loved ones. No one, and I mean no one, who has ever gone through such an experience could ever comprehend the degree of suffering and devastation that's inflicted.

"You know, they say that the loss of a child is the worst thing that could ever happen to a parent. And this is true. A parent who loses a child to, let's say, cancer or a horrible car accident, will never be the same. But as is the case with cancer, this is one of those things in life that sometimes can't be avoided. As with a car accident, a healthy person is here one second, and the next second they're dead. These situations where people happen to be in the wrong place at the wrong instant unfortunately happen. No one's immune from the possibility, unless they live in a cave or on a desert island. But usually, and I stress the word *usually*, the accidents aren't deliberate. Sometimes they aren't even the result of irresponsible behavior, like in the case of an irresponsible drunk driver. As the saying goes, 'Shit happens.'

"But now let's take the case of the murderer who rapes, sodomizes, and dismembers a little girl. This is now beyond the realm of an 'accident.' It's a deliberate act of unspeakable evil.

"You know, one time my mother was friends with a co-worker. This very thing happened to her only son. My mom went to the funeral to pay her respects. The woman's body was limp, and she wasn't able to walk under her own power. She had to be held up by two men on either side of her. It took all their effort just to keep her up as they dragged her down a corridor. All the while, tears were streaming down her face, and she was wailing, 'My baby! 'My baby!' I asked my mom, 'What do you say to someone at a time like this?' and she said, 'You don't say *anything*. You just hold them.'

"So, what I propose is to have mandatory sentences which are so severe that it'd be a deterrent to anyone who even *thought* about committing a similar crime. Would it eradicate the violent crime problem? Of course not. But if it saved just one victim who would've otherwise come to a violent end, had the criminal not thought twice about the punishment if he were caught, then it would've served its purpose.

"So, let's get down to specifics. The *family* of the victim, *not* the jurors who didn't know the victim, should decide on whether or not the perpetrator gets the death penalty. Personally, I have zero problem with taking the life of someone who would callously rob another of *their* life. And I've already mentioned the fact that their family and loved ones are now sentenced to a lifetime of pain and suffering that they'll *never* get over. Perhaps they'll be able to function again, but a void has been created in their lives that will always remain.

"But I do realize that some people, for religious reasons, are opposed to the death penalty, even when the ones they loved dearly were needlessly taken from them...hence, my assertion that the family and loved ones should determine whether the perpetrator gets the death penalty, as opposed to life in prison without the possibility of parole. As I just stated, I have no moral problem with the death penalty, but that being said, I personally think that a life behind bars under the most severe conditions is an even greater punishment. And yes, professor, I used the word *punishment*, and if you'd like to translate that to mean *revenge*, go ahead and do so.

"If life imprisonment is decided upon, then, as I mentioned, there'd be no possibility of parole. And this includes presidential pardons. The only rare exception to this sentence would be if it's subsequently determined by DNA evidence that the accused didn't commit the crime. But for the purposes of this discussion, let's assume that it's irrefutable that the person was guilty of the crime.

"They would be placed in solitary confinement. There would be no visitors, telephone calls, books, magazines, TV, or radio. The cell would have no windows, so that the person could never even have a glimpse of the outside world again. The cell would contain a toilet, a sink, and a mattress…nothing else. Once a week, a guard could hose down the prisoner if the smell became too offensive. They would not be allowed out of the cell for any reason. Three times a day, a meal would be slid through a slot at the bottom of the cell. Once a week, their clothes could be slid through the slot in order to be laundered.

"And one other thing, professor. Let's say, just for argument's sake, that the mandated severe punishment for violent, horrific crime were *not* a deterrent. At the very least, there'd be one less person in the world who could ever commit a horrific crime again. And don't dare try to say that criminals who didn't have to post bail and were let out of jail, often repeatedly, didn't then go on to commit other atrocities they wouldn't have been able to commit had they not been let loose. Because many of these cases have been documented.

"And by the way, professor, have you ever asked yourself if your views might in any way change if your wife were the victim of a violent criminal who committed other violent crimes but was repeatedly let loose?"

"No decent person likes violent crime, doctor. But your proposed punishments are barbaric. This isn't who we are. This would be like a Third World country or dictatorship. We don't torture people. Part of what differentiates us from the Putins and Assads of the world is our compassion."

"What about our compassion for the innocent victims?"

"If we resort to such cruel and inhuman punishment, we become no better than the ones we're punishing."

"Really, professor? Are you really saying there's a moral equivalent?"

"One of the purposes of incarceration, doctor, is something we've already discussed…rehabilitation. It's been demonstrated that convicted criminals who are treated inhumanely become even more angry and violent when they're let out."

"But in this case, professor, I don't think this is something society would have to worry about, be-cause—as I've already stated—these people would never *get* out. Nor should they. And regarding your characterization of the punishment I propose in response to horrific crimes, if they're barbaric and inhuman as you say, I have one iron-clad solution that would guarantee that no one would ever have to endure a life sentence under these conditions. Don't commit the crime."

"Well, one of my tenets, doctor—and this is how I live my life—is that in order to demonstrate we're more righteous than those who would harm us, we don't allow ourselves to fall to their level. We're not motivated by punishment or revenge, only love."

"Love?"

"If God can love these people, surely we can too."

"If your love is bestowed equally upon righteous good people and monsters, it says that your love is indiscriminate, and it therefore cheapens the very concept of what love is meant to represent. Love is something that should be *earned*, professor, not something that should be given out like candy on Halloween. When I love someone, I admire their values. I admire them because of who they are. I don't love someone just because they happened to have been born. The fact is, professor, that Vladimir Putin, Bashar al-Assad, Xi Jinping, Kim Jong-un, Mohammed bin Salman, Ali Khamenei, Jeffrey Dahmer, and people who've raped, sodomized, and murdered innocent people are pieces of shit."

"You know, doctor, I think this is a disgrace. A renowned psychologist and philosopher like yourself resorting to these characterizations is beneath you and beneath your profession."

"Really? Then tell me, professor, what *your* characterization of these people would be."

"Well, you don't go around calling people pieces of shit."

"Who is *you*? I know it's not *me*, because I just called them that. But perhaps I should have said 'misguided?' Or was the excuse for their bestiality due to their toilet training? Or perhaps it was because their friends didn't let them play with their toys when they were young?"

"I think this debate is an exercise in futility, doctor. I was expecting a woman of your reputation to at least be able to engage in a productive, rational discussion. But I guess I was wrong. It's a shame that all you can do is resort to childish name-calling. To God, *all* His creations hold equal value. He loves us all equally."

"How do you know?"

"Because we are all children of God, and God is not only omnipotent but omnibenevolent."

"What does it mean if His love is doled out equally to a saint and to a monster? If this were true, I would consider His values to be seriously screwed up."

"I thought I've already made it clear, doctor, that God's reasons are irrelevant. Whatever God chooses to do or not to do is right, because He's a supreme being. Therefore, His goodness is an irreducible primary, and we don't question His motives."

"You must not be including *me* when you say *we*, professor."

"You don't have the knowledge nor intelligence to grasp the meanings of a supreme being, doctor. You as a mere mortal are also limited by your five senses. That's all you have to go by."

"So I would assume, professor, that this would likewise refer to you as well, since you too are a mere mortal."

"Of course. I never suggested I wasn't."

"So if we're so limited, professor, how do *you* know all these things regarding God's motivations and the unconditional love you say He has for all His creations?"

"Sometimes, doctor, there are realms that transcend mere knowledge, rationality, and logic. It's called faith."

"Faith, by definition, professor, is belief in the absence of proof."

"I just told you, doctor; knowledge, rationality, and logic aren't everything. We don't have to analyze why we love someone. We know it when we feel it."

"Yes, professor, just like a baby knows they love their mother, and knows they *don't* love someone who would slap or abuse them. They don't have to grasp the concept as to 'why' they don't love that person. They're too young. But that doesn't mean their assessments are any less accurate. But when you refer to God, you're referring to something we cannot perceive with our senses. But people believe in Him anyway because of faith. And faith, as you indicated, doesn't require rationality and logic."

"That's right."

"It's interesting that a philosopher, of all people, would say this."

"I do believe in rationality and logic, doctor, but some things cannot always be explained. We, after all, are not solely intellectual beings. We possess a heart and feelings."

"So that means that sometimes when we don't know something, we conveniently invent a concept—in this case, God—to explain everything we don't know, and to have something convenient to fall back on when we're trying to win a debate."

"Doctor, God sent His only son down to Earth to die for our sins. This means that every sinner can achieve salvation. Only an infidel and a sinner could make such a statement."

"I've already indicated earlier that it's interesting that God sent His only son to Earth to be painfully murdered, and that God chose to sacrifice a higher being to save lesser beings and sinners. This doesn't seem to me like a very equitable swap. But if I'm an infidel and a sinner, professor, at least I feel better that I'm not going to Hell, because you just told me every sinner can achieve salvation. So I guess the only thing I'm really guilty of is being misguided.

"But until you can offer proof, professor, I don't accept what you consider to be irreducible primaries. When I observe things that don't make sense, that don't add up, I question them. I'm not obligated to prove a negative. If something is ethical because of some preconceived notion that a so-called supreme being can do no wrong, then I would require proof. That means I'd first need proof that a supreme being exists. Then I'd need proof that this means He could do no wrong. After all, Vladimir Putin, Bashar al-Assad, Kim Jong-un, Xi Jinping, Mohammed bin Salman, and Ali Khamenei are the supreme leaders of their countries. Otherwise, I'd just consider your assertions to be merely strategies to win an argument based on false premises."

"Are you comparing Vladimir Putin, Bashar al-Assad, Kim Jun-un, Xi Jinping, Mohammed bin Salman, and Ali Khamenei to God?"

"Not at all, professor. But they do. I don't care about your declarations as to the essence of God, whom you call a supreme being. I don't care about your conclusions regarding why we should never question things related to faith. I am, admittedly, a limited being, and therefore of limited capacity. I'm not as intelligent as I want to be, and I don't possess as much knowledge as I want. But I do know what pain and suffering is, and when I witness it, I ask, 'Why?' And if I can't come up with an answer, that doesn't mean I have to accept pain and suffering.

"And just because we're not omnipotent, that doesn't mean we can't come up with our own premises or irreducible primaries based on the knowledge we *have*. And one of mine is this: A person doesn't deserve to be hurt or be the recipient of aggression if they didn't try to hurt the perpetrator or another innocent person. If innocent people are hurt because of crimes such as robbery or vandalism, they're still being hurt by the criminal, even if they don't cross paths with him or her or know them.

"The only exception I'd make would be in situations in which people perished due to natural disasters such as hurricanes, tsunamis, earthquakes, forest fires, tornadoes, floods, mudslides, and volcanic eruptions. It could be argued that these are evil forces but, unlike people, they don't possess cognition and volition.

They're not creating their destruction to get even with anyone. Humans, however, *do* create destruction through malicious intent. Humans *do* perpetrate death and destruction because it gives them power over others...and to witness people suffering gives them pleasure. This is *my* definition of evil, professor.

"I was about to ask you if your compassion would extend to the people who would murder your wife and children if they were in Ukraine, and the murderers had been identified and caught. I could guarantee you, professor, that all your pious and intellectual platitudes you throw out to impress your students would change if these situations affected you personally.

"This reminds me of something Mike Tyson once said. He's no paragon of virtue and civility, but there was a lot of truth to it. He said, 'Everyone has a plan until they get punched in the face.'"

"Doctor, I think everything we've been discussing today indicates the fundamental difference between you and me. No one who's a proponent of your ideas or so-called solutions could ever be identified as someone who values and respects the sanctity and dignity of human life."

"Professor, it's precisely *because* of my value and respect for the sanctity and dignity of human life that I believe and advocate what I do."

Professor Markov was about to reply when a water beetle crawled into his line of vision. He suddenly lifted his foot and stamped out its life with a large thud. "What did you just do?" asked Mildred.

"Ah, a water beetle," replied Markov.

"Why did you kill it?"

"It was just a water beetle, doctor. So, we were discussing the sanctity of human life."

"What about the sanctity of all life, professor?"

"Doctor, are you ready to continue our discussion, or are you going to continue to waste time over an insignificant water beetle?"

"Insignificant, professor?"

"Doctor, it's just an insect, for God's sake."

"Professor, what does being a philosopher mean to you?"

"Well, on a basic level, doctor, it refers to people who think, who try to make sense of the universe, who ponder the meaning and ramifications of our existence, and try to prove whether there are *a priori* guidelines, not just empirical ones, regarding ethics.

We are people who search for the truth, and even if we can't determine it at a given time, at least we ask the right questions."

"Very well put, professor. I think you've captured the true essence of what a philosopher should be."

"Sometimes, doctor, an issue might not be totally clear on its surface. But often, when we uncover the layers through deductive reasoning, we come up with an answer, in the same manner as when someone is doing geometric proofs; one correct conclusion leads to another."

"Again, professor, I have to say that I couldn't have expressed that better myself. Why did you kill the water beetle?"

"Because it was dirty and ugly, and posed a distraction."

"I can't help thinking that there are many people who would fit that characterization."

"Yes, doctor, but in the hierarchy of living things, insects are a decidedly lower form of life."

"What, precisely, do you mean by 'lower form of life?'"

"Well, doctor, for one, they're nowhere near as anatomically advanced."

"Birds can fly, professor. Some of them can even swoop down and catch a fish a great distance away in the ocean. This is a great aerodynamic achievement. People can't fly by their own power. Dogs can hear pitches at frequencies people cannot. Their sense of smell is also far greater developed. People depend on dogs to help find drugs and catch criminals."

"Doctor, in reference to your example of the birds, humans can create vehicles that can defy gravity and fly, and can even go to the moon. A lower species could never do this, because they don't have the necessary brainpower."

"So I take it, professor, that intelligence is what separates 'higher' beings from 'lower' ones."

"Yes, doctor. Our brains and our power to think, reason, and form concepts."

"And that's what makes us higher beings?"

"Yes, doctor."

"So with that reasoning, should we conclude that people of high intelligence are higher forms of life than people of low intelligence?"

"No, doctor, because they're of the same species."

"So intelligence, professor, is not the only criteria?"

"No, doctor, it also has to do with anatomical complexity."

"I see. So from that, I gather that living things with less anatomical complexity are more expendable."

"I don't know if I would use the term *expendable*, doctor, but yes, if we kill an animal, it's less morally significant than if we kill a person."

"Professor, would you agree that dolphins and gorillas are some of the smartest mammals and primates, respectively?"

"Yes, I would agree with that, doctor. What's your point?"

"Would you agree that a highly intelligent dolphin or gorilla could be smarter than a severely intellectually disabled human?"

"I suppose that could be possible, doctor, but regarding people with severely low intelligence, this is an aberration; you're comparing a small subset of a species, which isn't the norm."

"So I take it that the example I just gave is not a very good one."

"I'm afraid not, doctor."

"Alright, professor, then with your arguments regarding anatomical complexity and intelligence, would I be correct in concluding that killing dogs, cows, pigs, cats, chickens, turkeys, and hens would be wrong and, especially in the case of dogs, even punishable, but killing insects would be less morally significant?"

"Yes, doctor."

"How about rodents such as rats, professor? Let's say there were a rat infestation in your home? What would you try to do about it?"

"I know what you're trying to get me to say, doctor. I would try to have them poisoned and eliminated, because rats pose a definite threat to humans. If they bite us, we can get sick, and in some instances even die. They live in filthy environments and are found where garbage is. They are dirty, disgusting, and vile creatures."

"They are examples of one of God's creations, professor. And if God created them, I'm sure He must've had a reason. And being that God is a supreme being, His reasons aren't important…or at least we shouldn't question them, because as you've stated, whatever God chooses to do is right solely by virtue of the fact that He's a supreme being. I'm using *your* words, professor. But I happen to totally agree with you. I'd certainly want to eradicate rats from the world, with the possible exception of those that are domesticated and serve as pets to some people, as they are filthy, vile creatures that can cause and spread disease and create major health hazards.

"I'd say the same regarding flies, as they live in shit and garbage. When I'm in a restaurant and one lands on my food, I can no longer enjoy my meal. When I'm home, even with a flyswatter at the ready, I can rarely catch one of them. But when I do, it makes me *very* happy, professor. And when I'm hiking and a mosquito bites me, I crush it with no moral dilemmas whatsoever. They've committed aggression against me, have sucked my blood, and there's always the chance I can get very sick, especially if I get Lyme disease from a tick bite.

"Rats, according to your definition, professor, are a 'higher' form of life than an insect. They're more anatomically advanced, and more intelligent. But I'd eradicate them with as much alacrity as I'd eradicate flies and mosquitos. But do you know what? Rats are also much more anatomically advanced than ladybugs. But when I see one, I take a piece of paper, gently lift it up, and take it outside to their environment...which is exactly what *I* would've done with the water beetle you killed.

"In order to be intellectually honest, professor, I'm not totally morally off the hook myself. I do eat cow, chicken, turkey, and duck, and I'm aware that many of these animals live under barbarically inhumane conditions and are slaughtered the same way. People, including myself, have rationalized that if they ate grass-fed meat, the animals weren't treated as inhumanely. But they're still being killed nonetheless. We also rationalize that animals eat other animals in order to survive, even though humans don't have to eat meat in order to survive. But then we continue to rationalize that many animals would kill *us* for food if they had the chance, so we shouldn't feel morally wrong to eat *them* for survival...even though, as I've already said, people can live very well on a plant-based diet.

"In addition, millions of people all over the world eat meat, to the point that it's universally accepted. No one passes judgment on me when I order chicken parmesan in a restaurant. But that doesn't make it right, just because 'everyone else does it.' I also wear leather shoes, have leather pocketbooks, and the keys on my piano are made of ivory. I'd never hunt for sport, but that does *not* make me right for doing the other things I admitted to. I have, in fact, been discussing all these things with my husband recently, and weighing everything in my mind. I don't regard hypocrisy as an admirable trait, and I believe that as a philosopher, I owe it, at least to myself, to live by my convictions - not just when it's convenient to do so.

"The point I'm trying to make, professor, is that animals feel pain just like we do, and that less 'intelligent' and 'anatomically advanced' animals often cause far less pain and suffering than humans, the so-called 'higher' beings. Is a rapist and serial killer really a higher form of life than an insect? If not, why would it be more morally wrong to kill the former than the latter? A serial killer might be more 'anatomically' advanced as you put it, but who poses a greater threat to you, a rat and an insect or a serial killer? And if, by some dispensation, we could eradicate all serial killers with the push of a button, wouldn't it be more advantageous than eradicating the rats and insects if we had a choice?

"Professor, have you ever thought about what the purpose of a zoo is? It's to have animals in a cage, not in their natural habitat, so that people can gawk at the 'lower beings,' and so little girls can say, 'Mommy, look at the gorilla!' I've often daydreamed about violent criminals being similarly displayed in a zoo: Now we're going to the 'rapist cage,' and now we're going to the 'serial killer cage.' Relax, professor, I'm not saying I'm advocating this. I'm just saying that if you're intellectually honest, why would it be less ethical to similarly display a serial killer than a gorilla? I certainly wouldn't consider it to be.

"Professor, when we came here today for our friendly 'debate,' I really didn't want to consider it as such, but rather a discussion. Debates imply winners and losers. Discussions should be about exchanging ideas. Sometimes in a debate—political ones are prime examples—even if one person is checkmated, they'll never admit it. They have to 'save face' at all costs. A politician will almost *never* admit they lied. If they shot someone to death right in front of everyone, they'd say it was an optical illusion.

"I'm not here to prove you wrong, and vice versa. I'm here to try to discover truth. And as I've told my patients, when someone checkmates me, I'm happy in a way, because I've learned something. I may not have 'won' the debate, but I discovered a better way to think about something. And if I'm being intellectually honest, I'd expect that my integrity dictates that I admit my mistake.

Again, professor, I'm not trying to prove your ideas wrong. I'd just hope that when you state your convictions, you've analyzed the reasons and not come to your conclusions based on what everyone was 'brought up' to believe, because everyone else believes it, or because it's the 'right' or 'proper' thing to believe. Believe something when you have evidence from your senses, and when your own rational judgment dictates to you that it's true. And I'll try to do the same." Mildred and Irwin Markov then shook hands.

George approached Mildred backstage to congratulate her. "George," she replied, "as I was saying regarding having someone proving me wrong, it doesn't happen very often, but it has with Leroy."

"Who's Leroy?"

"Leroy's a dirty and smelly homeless man who was once begging in front of Grand Central. I took him to Carnegie Deli for a meal, then took him home with me, so he could shower and get into fresh, clean clothes."

"You picked up a homeless man in the street and took him home with you?!"

"That's right. He was a philosophy professor who was down on his luck. He was also my greatest teacher."

CHAPTER FIVE

One of the people in the audience at Mildred's and Professor Markov's debate was Tony. Maria had been out of town visiting a relative. At the end of the debate, Tony approached Mildred, gave her a hug and a kiss, and congratulated her. "You know something, honey? I've heard about you, and read all about you, but I've never seen you in action. I just want to say that both Maria and I are very proud that you and Jim are our friends."

"Thank you so much, Tony. I don't think we have to tell you that we feel the same way about you."

Tony then joined Mildred and Jim for dinner in Little Italy. During dinner, Mildred asked Tony if he were okay. "I should know I'd never be able to get anything past someone like you," said Tony. "Yes, I do actually have something that's been bothering me. But I don't believe in dumping my problems on others. People have enough problems of their own."

"Tony, if two people are related, in a relationship, or friends, and one party has nothing else to offer but using the other person as a dumping ground for all their problems, I can see how that might be a problem, especially if the other person can't be of any help.

I could then construe that they're abusing the other person, even if that wasn't their intention. Don't get me wrong, Tony. The aforementioned *are* there to be supportive, caring, and understanding. But I want *good* things to be shared, too. This in no way implies that there aren't legitimate reasons why someone is troubled, angry, frustrated, depressed, or any other adjectives you can think of. But other than a situation where someone is my patient, and I'm *paid* to listen to their problems, if all I hear from this person are bad things, and if good things are never shared, I begin to question whether this person's attitude, mindset, and sense of life are contributing to their woes.

"I know, Tony, that you'd never take advantage of our friendship by deliberately imposing on me in any way. But I asked you what was wrong, not out of curiosity, but out of selfish concern. You see, if you're not happy, I'm not happy. So what I'm trying to say, with this big lecture I've just given you, is that you wouldn't be imposing on me in any way."

"Thank you, honey. I really appreciate it."

"Why don't we go to my office after dinner?"

"Oh, don't worry, Mildred. You don't have to speak with me tonight. It's not an emergency or anything."

"I know I don't have to, Tony, but I offered this to you as your friend, so you can erase any guilt you may have out of your mind. If someone's in pain, why should they postpone doing something that could possibly make them feel better?"

Tony went back to Mercer Street with Mildred and Jim. Upon arriving, she prepared some hot chocolate with whipped cream, and Tony followed her to her office, where they both sat down. "So, what is it, Tony?"

"Okay. When I was a kid, my mother got me two guinea pigs. One day I wanted to clean the cage, so I picked one of them up. As I was doing so, she squirmed and tried to break free. I don't know where it came from, but in a flash of anger I threw her down to the floor. Right after that, I noticed she was limping. Her leg was broken. My mom noticed it too, and thought the other guinea pig had attacked her. She even scolded and hit her, and said, 'Bad girl.' I didn't tell my mom I was the one responsible.

"Anyway, we took her to the vet, and they put a cast on her leg. We took the other pig along too, because she was getting so fat and we couldn't figure out why. The vet said, 'Don't feed her so much.' We brought them home, and the next day I come home after school and the 'fat' guinea pig is giving birth to two baby guinea pigs. My mom, for whatever reason, decided she didn't want the responsibility anymore, so she gave them to a children's museum where they had pets. Then I heard that the guinea pig I hurt was put to sleep.

"Now, that being said, let me go off on a tangent for a moment. Mildred, we all know the prevalence of scams going on these days. It's getting worse and worse. And I'm not just referring to the emails we get from descendants of the royal family of Nigeria. There's the romance scams, such as the cryptocurrency ones, in which someone finds you on Facebook or texts you, sends you a picture of a beautiful woman, and insists on only texting with you or communicating on WhatsApp. Then the woman, or a man posing as one, slowly gets more and more romantic, starts calling you 'honey,' 'darling,' and 'sweetheart,' and says they want to be with you. Then the cryptocurrency thing gets mentioned. They tell you their father taught them how to make a fortune, tells them when to make transactions, and even sends you balance sheets to 'prove' it. Then they want to be your 'teacher' so you'll then have enough money to be with her forever, and never have to worry about money again.

"And then there's the Russian dating scams. It's all planned and built up like a novel. They're finally going to come to the US to be with you forever. But at the last minute...well, you know the story. Anyway, one time me and Maria are watching a news program. This sweet old lady forked over her whole life savings, her late husband's pension, the proceeds of the sale of her house, and was left destitute. Add this to the fact that she never got the 'love' she thought would come into her life from this wonderful 'gentleman.' And if this weren't enough, she had cancer, and the insurance wouldn't cover her astronomical payments for chemotherapy.

"So me and Maria are watching this and we're both crying like a baby. I told Maria, 'I got to find that motherfucker.' But if we contacted the woman, how would she know I wasn't just another scammer ready to take over where the other guy left off? But we contact her, I told her to bring her lawyer there at the same time, and had to use all my powers of persuasion to convince them I wasn't who they suspected I might be.

"Anyway, the scammer resurfaced a few weeks later, and ended up contacting her for *more* money. That's when me and my guys took over. It took about four months, but we finally tracked him down and met him face-to-face in France. To make a long story short, we took care of him. And before we did, we also managed to recover a large portion of what he stole, and returned it to the lady. When we witnessed her shocked reaction, it was one of the greatest days of my life."

"How did you then feel about taking care of the scammer?"

"Do you mean did I have any 'moral' problems with what we did? Not at all, Mildred. It was like drinking a glass of water. And meanwhile, after all these years, I can't live with myself over what I did to that cute, little, innocent guinea pig."

"Thank you for sharing this with me, Tony. You know, everyone's done something wrong at one time or another. One of the laws of logic states that when something has happened, it cannot then *un*happen. But if we know it's wrong, try to make reparations, and never do it again, then the incident doesn't define us as a person. I'm no different than you. One time, a bee was flying around. I swatted at it and miraculously caught it right in my hand. In the microseconds that followed, I had the option of letting it go or crushing it. If I crushed it, I'd have accomplished the 'feat' of killing a bee in one fell swoop of my hand. But if I let it go, I wouldn't have accomplished my 'feat.' So I immediately crushed its life out. I then tried to rationalize that bees sting people, and that I've been stung by bees. But this bee didn't sting me, and there was no reason I should've killed it.

"Tony, when you threw down that guinea pig, you were mad. You immediately realized you were wrong, and have been carrying around this guilt and pain with you all these years. If you didn't have a 'heart,' you wouldn't have carried these emotions with you. That, of course, didn't prevent her from getting a broken leg. But she was taken to the vet, and a cast was put on it. When people break a leg, Tony, do you know what happens when they get a cast put on and it finally heals? It gets stronger. That's probably what would've happened with *her*. If she *were* put to sleep, it wasn't your decision, and you had no control over it. All you wanted was for her leg to heal. And if she weren't taken to the museum, you would have loved her, nurtured her, fed her, taken care of her, and given her nothing but tenderness.

"Tony, I want you to buy two guinea pigs, so that both will have a companion and not be lonely by themselves. Preferably, it should be a male and a female, so that possibly the female will get pregnant and give birth to more guinea pigs. Keep them in a big cage so they'll have plenty of room, feed them well, get a treadmill wheel so they'll have recreation and something to play with, take care of them, pet them, and give them all your love. And try to frequently let them *out* of the cage so it's not like they're in prison."

Tony stared at Mildred, and she smiled gently. Then he held her tight. "I love you," he said.

"I love you, too," she replied.

* * *

The following Monday, George met Mildred for another session on Mercer Street. Before they both got settled in her office, Jim arrived. "Hi, honey," he said to Mildred, giving her a kiss. "Oh, hi George," he added while shaking his hand. "How are you doing?"

"How was your day, sweetie?" asked Mildred.

"Ach, I have to go upstairs to shower and change. I shit in my pants today." He threw his hands in the air dismissively and walked out of the room.

George looked at Mildred. "I can't believe he just said that."

"What's the matter, haven't you ever shit in your pants?"

"Yes, but I don't go announcing it to the world. I'd think that's something you'd want to keep to yourself."

"Yeah, most people feel the same way. But Jim's very open. He doesn't give a shit—no pun intended—what anyone thinks. He's not ashamed that he's human, and that's one of the things I love about him. The fact is, George, everyone's shit in their pants at one time or another. Everyone's had diarrhea, vomited, farted, even Victoria's Secret models and math geniuses."

When they were seated in her office, Mildred asked how he was doing. "I could be better, Mildred," he replied. "The fact is, I think I'm wasting a lot of time. I feel I do a lot of things I shouldn't be doing. And when I do buckle down and start working on a piece I want to polish and memorize, I start thinking I should be working on another piece, or that I'm spending too much time on one thing. Then I start thinking that maybe I should go to the gym to work out. That should be like brushing my teeth and taking a shower every day. I tell myself I'll start tomorrow. Or I'll go to a restaurant to order something I'm really craving, and tell myself I'll begin my strict diet and exercise regimen tomorrow. Often, they're out of the food I want, so I give myself permission to have what I was craving the

next time I'm out. I'll start my regimen the day after
that. It's a vicious cycle, and it never ends."

"That's completely normal. Many people wrestle
with these same issues. What's destructive is when they
become a lifelong pattern. I once had a well-known
violinist for a patient who struggled with these same
issues. Because he was self-employed, the temptations
present when he was home interfered with the intense
practicing he should've been doing. He ended up eating to deal with his boredom, surfing the internet, and
watching the same commercial on the TV for the mil-
lionth and first time, even though he vowed never to
subject himself to this again.

"Well, I don't feel that asking a patient how their
week went is usually the most important question I
should ask. Everyone in the world has bad days. Their
car breaks down; they get stuck in a terrible traffic jam;
they step in shit on the way to an important interview;
a waitress is rude to them. If I asked a patient to reit-
erate all the petty annoyances that are a normal part of
life, we'd be losing track of the larger picture.

"Don't get me wrong, George. These things aren't
pleasant, and I don't wish to downplay them. But an
evolved and confident person with high self-esteem is
far less immobilized by the less important challenges

in life, whereas a person of lesser self-esteem will often let something fester and grow like a cancer...much like you let happen with the Poker Queen. The person of high self-esteem realizes that life is too short to keep thinking about a worthless piece of shit. They cut their losses, vow never to spend any more of their precious time dwelling on it and thinking about that person, and move on. Their life is too important to do otherwise. If you dwell on the unpleasant things in the past, George, it means you're not living in the present.

"Now, you might be asking what all this has to do with the situation you brought up. But it's all related. The fact is, George, time is a limited commodity. That's one of those cliches that *is* true. Now, one of the things I always try to do as a therapist is to implement *workable* solutions with my patients. We don't need to spend a whole session discussing that someone's mother always unjustly criticized them, put them down, and made them angry. I don't mean to downplay the significance of things like that. And I understand that sometimes these things are the genesis of future, long-lasting problems because they're internalized, even if the patient doesn't realize it. But we can't go back in time like an episode of *The Twilight Zone*. I think it's far more important to deal with the *now*, George. What can I do *now* to make the best use of my time? A parent or someone else might've done something wrong to you in the past. But why help them out, and let another person—namely yourself—continue the job you allowed others to start?

"You know, George, about three years ago, I was at a cocktail party, and one of the people I was introduced to asked what I did for a living. I told him I was a psychologist. He then asked me what my fee was, even though he wasn't inquiring for himself or a relative or acquaintance as a possible patient, and even though he wasn't my accountant. Sometimes, when someone asks you how much money you make, it's to compare themselves to you. If they charge more than you do, especially if they're in the same field, they'll respond, 'Very reasonable,' indicating they make more than you do and making you feel inferior at the same time.

"But anyway, for whatever reason, rather than telling him 'none of your damn business,' I told him my actual rate of 300 dollars per session. His response was, 'Well, I think you're a big rip-off artist.' I know I should always consider the source, but I was very hurt. He viewed us 'shrinks' as an indulgence for rich people, because it was the fashionable thing to do, and that we essentially rationalized their terrible behavior by explaining that them not shitting fast enough during potty training had made their mommy angry. The fact is, George, there *are* therapists like that. But I take my job very seriously, and can assert that there've been moments of catharsis I've experienced with patients, moments when I saw a light go on over their head, and moments of life-changing revelation. I've also observed incredible transformations. And that's what I live for.

"Now, let's get down to some specifics…and these are strategies I've explored with the violinist. He had an important engagement coming up, where he was booked to play the Brahms Concerto. But he kept procrastinating with his practicing, which served a dual purpose. If he gave a poor performance at the concert, he could blame it on all the time he was wasting, not because he was a bad violinist. So, we instituted what I called the 'work-around' strategy. Every day he procrastinated like this, he was to designate time solely for drop-dead work on the concerto. During this period, nothing else in the world existed. He was not to answer the phone, a doorbell, or to stop work for any reason whatsoever. It didn't matter how bored he might feel. It didn't matter how tired he was, how depressed he was, or how much he didn't feel like doing it.

"He started doing this for an hour a day. He would jot the time he was starting down on a piece of paper, and he *always* ended up accomplishing more than he thought he would…and always felt better afterwards. Since one hour worked so well, we added another hour session at whatever part of the day he chose. He could work on the concerto if more work were needed, or he could choose to spend some or all of this time on another piece he wanted to perform in the future, so long as the same conditions applied. Similarly, he could do whatever he wanted *around* his work when the hour was completed.

"Well, sometimes he became so engrossed in what he was doing that he ended up exceeding his hour sessions. He didn't want to stop until he achieved a particular task. Rather than making a blanket resolution as to what he'd do, we eased into these new behaviors gradually. If one is thinking about other things they should be doing, they're not focusing on the task at hand, and are undermining its effectiveness.

"You know, George, about all those stupid New Year's resolutions people make. 'I'm going to stop smoking at the stroke of midnight on December 31, so until that time I'll smoke like a chimney.' Or, 'I'm going to lose weight by eating a spartan diet and exercising like hell, so I'll fill up on bacon double cheeseburgers until the stroke of midnight to get it all out of my system. Then I'll wave a magic wand.' As you know, these strategies almost never work. They're all gung ho for about a week, then all their strategies go to hell.

"The fact is, if you're a bodybuilder training for Mr. Olympia, and the competition is coming up, every single thing you put in your body has to be scrutinized. You're not going to risk not winning, and missing out on fame and fortune, because you went to a birthday party and didn't want to hurt Aunt Millie's feelings by not eating her world's greatest chocolate cheesecake.

"So, in regard to the violinist, or to you, you gradually increase your drop-dead intense sessions. You eventually segue into writing down specific times to set aside for work and for work only...not only with your piano practice, which is vitally important to you, but with other things that are almost equally important, like your fitness regimen.

"How do you prioritize? Well, not everyone's the same, and everyone has different priorities. If you were the bodybuilder training for Mr. Olympia, you'd probably have to live, eat, and sleep fitness and training 24/7. You'd almost have to live in the gym. That wouldn't leave you much time for piano, but that wouldn't matter to most bodybuilders. So, the answer regarding what to prioritize is based on *you* and only you can answer that question, as everyone's different. Many people can benefit by going to a shrink, but a shrink usually doesn't need to tell that person what they're passionate about. They can guide a person to realize what their passions are; they can implement specific strategies for maximizing the realization and achievement of their goals; but they can't tell them what to value, what to be passionate *about*, what to live and wake up in the morning for. That's something you have to discover, even if that means having someone else help you discover it.

"You told me twice before that you don't care that you're not, nor ever could be, as good a basketball or tennis player as Michael Jordan or Novak Djokovic respectively, because basketball and tennis are not your top priorities in life. I happen to have excelled in philosophy, because I felt it'd help me as a psychologist. The studying and research I've done, and continue to do, is enormous. Could I have still succeeded if I didn't work quite as hard? Yes. But I wouldn't have been as good as I could be…not to say I'm good. There are still many things I have to learn and discover—the meaning of dreams, for instance, and the means by which we can record our dreams as if by videotape.

"But the fact is, George, everyone can't be an expert in everything, and every person in the world has to deal with the same fact of life, namely time, that limited commodity. It's really a bitch, but the more of it we waste, the less of it we have. When you waste your time, you're wasting part of your life.

"Jim will tell you I'm a lousy cook. I could kill him for saying so, but he's right. I always thought that as a woman and wife, part of the 'job' was to be a good cook. But you know what, George? This is of little interest to me, and this isn't how I want to spend my time.

"Now, that doesn't mean I don't love to eat. I *love* to eat…that is, I love to eat *other* people's recipes. And I love cake, ice cream, chocolate, and all the other naughty things you could mention. Am I fat? Yes. Would I like to be slim? Yes. But I'm not willing to give up what I love, even if it means that I die two years sooner.

"Being slim and fit and having a bikini-model body isn't my priority in life, because the things I love and enjoy supersede it. We all have to activate our own personal 'weight and balance scales,' as one self-help guru puts it.

"I once had an obese comedian for a patient. He was always depressed that he could never land a hot fitness chick, which was his greatest sexual fantasy. So he rationalized that all the women who turned him down were shallow and didn't recognize his brilliance. And he *did* happen to be a brilliant comic. He even used his weight as a main component of his act. Jim and I went to some of his performances, and we've rarely laughed so hard in our lives. He acted the role he wanted to portray to a T, just like if Woody Allen didn't look the way he did, *his* performances wouldn't have been quite so brilliant.

"But offstage, he was a profoundly unhappy and depressed man. I told him it was fine for him to want to be in a relationship, marry, or even just fuck a fitness babe, but reality states that fitness babes can get any man they want. They're not going to date an obese man unless he were very wealthy or famous. And it wasn't my job to agree with him that all those women who turned him down were 'shallow.' Maybe they were, and maybe it's unjust. But that didn't change the fact that he slept alone every night.

"What I *did* tell him was that he already had *some* of the ingredients. He was highly intelligent, and one of the most brilliant and creative comedians I'd ever seen. He was also quite good-looking, although you'd never realize it behind all that blubber. So I told him that if he wanted to land fitness babes, he'd have to *work* for it so he could be in their league. He then said to me that he was willing to hire a personal trainer, live in the gym, live, eat and sleep fitness when he's not writing his comedy acts, give up all the shit he ate, and instead eat organic non-GMO food, scrutinize everything he put in his body, and work out like a maniac every single day. 'But,' he asked me, 'what if, after a year, I do get a slim, fit, killer body with six-pack abs, but still can't get a fitness babe?'

"I asked him if he were asking me to issue him a guarantee. I told him I'm a therapist, not a wing woman." Mildred laughed. "I then asked him, 'What would you prefer—to have a slim, fit body and sleep alone, or to be obese and sleep alone?' He got the point. But I did tell him that if he were seriously willing to pay the price to get the body he wanted, I'd help guide him to achieve the love he so coveted, the lack of which created such a void in his life. But I stressed that before he embarked on his fitness journey, he should make sure he was doing it for himself first and that it conformed with his own values and priorities. Then, any positive things that resulted from this would be fantastic, but only fringe benefits. The biggest benefit would be what he gave him*self*…namely, the self-image he wanted to portray. How about you, George? Would you want that kind of incredible body?"

"As I told you regarding basketball and tennis, that's not my top priority. But unlike those things, I *could* actually have that kind of killer body with six-pack abs if I spent all my time in the gym. But if I did, I wouldn't have the time to excel at the most important thing I'm passionate about, namely my music. This is what defines *me* as a person. This is what I live for. So, for that reason, I'll never possess that kind of body. This doesn't mean I won't maintain a good body, better than most men my age. But I'm not willing to pay the price to get to that next level."

"This is good. You already know what one of your top priorities are. Many don't and just end up floundering in mindless activities that waste their most valuable commodity. But getting back to my patient, he actually *did* follow through on his diet and fitness journey. The transformation was absolutely astonishing. But he still wasn't landing the fitness babes he thought he wanted. Part of that had to do with his shyness, which you wouldn't believe he had when you saw him perform. But his offstage persona was completely different than what he portrayed *on*stage.

"We worked on various strategies, and I gave him homework to do...like when he came to session one day gushing over the drop-dead gorgeous woman who worked out at the gym the same time he did. He wanted her desperately, but was afraid to ask her out. I asked him if he wanted me to deliver her to him on a silver platter. He told me he was too scared to ask her out, because she'd never say yes, and then he'd feel embarrassed and humiliated. So his homework was to ask her out anyway. He did, and I then congratulated him on having the courage to do so, even though he was afraid. I stressed, as I do to all my patients, that constructive change and growth involve risk...and I'm not talking about 'gambling in Vegas' kind of risk. I'm talking about constructive risk. I told him that even if she said no, it'd make the next challenge a little easier.

"Well, as it turned out, she was in a relationship. She didn't reject him as a person, even though he didn't get the date. And do you know what? The sun still came up the next day, and the world didn't come to an end. Anyway, to make a long story short, he's now engaged...and *not* to a fitness babe. She's very pretty but not the kind of woman he always obsessed about in his mind's eye. But what she lacks in the way of a bikini-model body, she makes up for with her brilliant mind, killer sense of humor, enthusiasm for life, *joie de vivre*, and all the other million and one things that make her what she is. You see, George, when my patient weighed everything on his own balance scale, she came out ahead.

"I'm always challenging my patients to step out of their comfort zones. I had another highly talented pianist for a patient who experienced paralyzing nervousness onstage. We agreed that the only way to ameliorate this problem was to keep going *out* onstage. But I reminded him that he'd better make sure he was putting in the savage preparation, monk-like discipline, and necessary practice. That way, when he walked out into the floodlights, he knew he had done all he could. I also reminded him that a major component to fear onstage is related to self-esteem. We're more concerned about others' evaluations than our own.

"We were discussing time management as a road to maximizing your effectiveness by prioritizing what you deem to be most important in your life. As you know, George, if an airline is scheduled to leave the terminal at 8:57 p.m., they don't care if you got stuck in traffic or that your connecting flight was late. They don't care that you have a wedding or a funeral to attend. They leave anyway. Your work should be viewed in the same way. Gradually, little by little, the other frivolous shit gets eased out of your life. And do you know what, George? By that time, you don't even miss it.

"And do you know what else, George? Carrying excess baggage in your head weighs you down, just as if you were carrying a twenty-pound sack on your head. Spending excess time focusing on pieces of shit like the Poker Queen, or the guy who gave you the finger because you didn't accelerate from the red light fast enough for him, is all excess baggage. Clutter that fills up your head. Space that could be much better filled with important things. So, wasted time is very similar to having destructive thoughts. They're both forms of clutter. George, what is the goal of a great piano professor?"

"He's there to pass on the knowledge he's gained from *his* professors and experience. He's also there to constructively criticize me, so I can improve as a pianist and as a musician, and to see to it that I always strive to be better. But ultimately, the goal is to make me musically self-sufficient. I'll still encounter challenges, but I'll now have the tools to solve my own problems and figure things out for myself."

"That's right. It's just like a mother bird teaching her young ones to catch worms. Once they have the tools to survive, it's time to leave the nest. This is how I view my profession, George. Things come up, crises happen, and people can see me to help them deal with things like divorces and deaths of loved ones. But ultimately, just like the piano professor, I want to help my patients become *psychologically* self-sufficient. I'm not here to solve their problems, George. I'm here to help my patients solve their own problems, or at least deal with them. I can guide them, but I can't do the work for them.

"You know, the specifics of challenges might be different, but an evolved person of high self-esteem will almost always deal with these challenges better than someone with no self-esteem. And there's another famous saying that I like very much: 'If you give a man a fish, he can live another day. If you teach a man to fish, he can live a lifetime.'"

"Mildred, you mentioned that once time-wasting things get pushed out of your life by highly constructive things, eventually you don't have time for the frivolous things. But what about 'everything in moderation?'"

"Ah, another one of those bullshit sayings uttered so often that people don't even question it…partly, because like the 'beauty is in the eye of the beholder' quote, there are elements of truth in it. Yes, George, if you're a fitness maniac, a slice of chocolate cheesecake or pizza once in a while won't hurt you. But if you take fentanyl one time, it can kill you. And 'everything in moderation' also does *not* mean we can occasionally disregard our moral code. We can make a mistake, make an error in judgment—everyone does—but we don't do something that violates what we consider to be wrong. That's known as having *integrity*.

"I once saw someone in the audience of a well-known speaker at a college. He was railing about the injustice of affirmative action. When it was pointed out to this person that the only reason *he* was accepted to this university was because of affirmative action, he was caught in a trap and ended up floundering around, trying to make up lame rationalizations. The speaker wiped the floor with him, and exposed him for the hypocrite he was. He told him that if he was so upset about the injustice of affirmative action, he should leave the college. And he was absolutely right.

"Similarly, if someone preaches about the injustice of killing animals, this is fine as well, and there's a lot of truth to their proclamations as well as good reasons for *not* harming animals. But if you believe this, then be a vegan for life, not just when it's convenient to do so. And don't be wearing leather shoes and buying leather couches.

"I was once at a camp when I was a kid, and a girl told us she didn't believe in killing animals and eating meat. When we asked her why she ate fish, she said, 'They have less of a chance of becoming extinct.' Another kid said he was sure the fish she was eating would be glad to know that."

"And what did the girl say?"

"She didn't say anything. She just farted. But when she spoke, it was no different than farting out of her mouth."

"Mildred, we had been discussing labeling ourselves due to comparison. What does a pianist do if he feels that someone is better than he? If someone plays golf or cooks better than I do, I couldn't care less. But if someone plays a piece on the piano much better than I do, it really bothers me."

"Because your greatest passion is music and piano playing, and because your whole self-image is defined by how well you do something that you *do* want to be great at."

"That's right. I once heard a nine-year-old prodigy play 'Feux follets' on YouTube. It was astonishing. I couldn't believe the human hand was capable of playing with such speed and accuracy, let alone by a nine-year-old. And this piece—Liszt's Transcendental Etude

No. 5—is considered to be one of the most insanely difficult pieces ever written. Even Rachmaninoff and Horowitz thought so. It was as fast as Kissin's famous performance, which is one of those miracles that drive almost every other pianist to despair."

"Jealousy and envy are two of those wasted emotions, George. People who envy other people wish the object of their envy were not as good, so it wouldn't hurt *their* self-esteem. But like I've already told you, George, it's a contradiction. One's self-esteem is just that. It comes from the *self*, not from anyone else.

And people play subtle games with themselves and others all the time. I once heard a pianist play a concert at another pianist's house. Before the concert, I saw her outside and she said, 'I should've practiced more.' What do you think she meant by this, George?"

"I really don't know what you're getting at, Mildred."

"Well, here's why she said it. She said it to alleviate pressure and nervousness. If she didn't play well, then it wouldn't have been due to her not being a good pianist; it would've been because she didn't practice enough. And I—or whoever else she said this to— would feel the same way for the same reason. As it turned out, she played marvelously. But her comment served as her 'safety net.'

"But getting back to what we were discussing, people discriminate due to envy all the time, whether consciously or unconsciously. I heard a lawyer once say that a stunning woman on the witness stand will often be burned at the stake. Sometimes, a woman will see a gorgeous female newscaster on TV. Her good looks are a threat to her self-esteem, or lack thereof. She might describe her to a friend as a slut if she wears short skirts, or be happy if she hears that she's going through a painful divorce. A pianist might hear another pianist who they consider to be far superior to them, but will be glad that the other pianist is obese and ugly and they're not. You see, they need that detail to grasp onto. Then they can console themselves that maybe they'd rather be a less accomplished pianist and not obese and ugly than vice versa. We all have, at one time or another, been guilty of this, myself included. I am not now, nor was I ever, a beauty queen. But you know how cruel kids can be. I certainly exceeded my quota in terms of the comments that were made to me and the way I was treated. And it hurt, George."

"So what did you do about it?"

"I told myself that people are *not* created equal. Look at the obituaries. The ages that people die are all across the board. Is it fair that some people live thirty or forty years longer than others? No, it isn't. But it's reality...and reality isn't something we can—or I should say, *should* judge as being unfair. It simply is, and all the complaining in the world won't do anything to change it. The important thing is to make the best possible use of the time we *have*.

"A person who dies at fifty but discovered the cure for a disease, rescued animals, influenced people through whatever work they did, and left a wonderful legacy, has lived a more important life than the person who died at ninety, but spent most of their life watching TV, hanging out in a bar, playing Bingo, and going bowling. Now, is there anything immoral about spending your life doing this? No. But I think you'd agree that the former person lived a more substantial and productive life.

"I told myself I wouldn't dwell on the physical hand I was dealt, but instead would maximize other things. And I think I've done that, and continue to do so. But does that mean I never judge? No. I've already mentioned this to you. But just like what I mentioned regarding tennis players playing the ball rather than a person, you should view a magnificent performance as a standard to aspire to, rather than a goal to be better than a particular individual. Become as good as you possibly can be at things that are important to you by constantly elevating your skill and knowledge. Strive for *your* ideal *standard*. Even if we never reach that elusive standard, the striving to do so constantly elevates our level.

"And speaking of 'Feux follets,' one of the concert pianists who play in our music soirées here lamented that he never considered himself a great virtuoso. He played Bach, Beethoven, Mozart, Schubert, Schumann, and Brahms marvelously; and goodness knows, these pieces provide endless musical and interpretive mountains to summit, in *addition* to technical ones. But he always felt something was lacking in himself. His teacher pointed out that he'd heard fabulous performances by pianists in virtuoso pieces that never came close to demonstrating the musicality, intelligence, and command of structure in other repertoire that this pianist did. But unfortunately—and this is one of those facts of life—the general public responds more to finger-splitting displays of virtuosity than it does to profound musical interpretation. Someone who breaks the world speed record in 'The Flight of the Bumblebee' will elicit greater hysterical applause than the pianist who's just played a sublime performance of Beethoven's Sonata Opus 10, No. 3, for example, which, as you know, has one of the most incredible, gut-wrenching, and touching slow movements in the entire literature.

"His teacher at the time told him to learn 'Feux follets.' The pianist thought he was crazy, but he set about learning it anyway. He remembered what the great pianist Earl Wild had said about this piece: 'It's very difficult; that's all I can tell you. You can't just learn it and play it. It has to become a part of you.' How right he was! The pianist spent months practicing and memorizing it, and then began trying it out in front of one or two friends, then small audiences, then at concerts. At the beginning, he failed miserably. But then he devised different fingerings, isolated certain treacherous spots, and drilled them in sundry different ways. Slowly but gradually, the piece started to evolve. It became a *part* of him. Now he can play it at an almost world-class level. So there you have it…a pianist who considered himself to be lacking as a virtuoso, eventually being able to play one of the hardest pieces ever written." They both smiled.

"And one other thing, George. Never place anyone above you because of perceived status. That's also a tenet of self-esteem. Judge someone because of their accomplishments, not because of their position or title. You can fool others, and unfortunately you can even fool yourself. But that doesn't alter the reality. One need not look any further than Joe Biden, the most powerful and famous man in the world. He probably actually *believes* he's a great president. How else could such an utterly abysmal and totally incompetent and corrupt fool live with himself? Sadly, he has legions of admirers, but they don't admire *him*; they admire the man they *think* he is.

"Mildred, you've been telling me how important it is to have self-esteem. One's opinion about oneself is certainly more important than anyone else's. I do understand the benefits, and I do understand that one's self-esteem is based very often on our decision to always treat ourself with respect. But what if someone legitimately feels they're lacking in an area that is very important to them?"

"I can't help thinking that you're speaking about yourself, George." He looked down at the floor and nodded.

"Please...say what's on your mind. There's no need to sugarcoat anything here."

"I'm feeling that I'm stupid."

"Why?"

"Because there are so many things that other people can do and I can't. I'm dependent on others for everything, and have difficulty understanding and retaining things. I feel that if I took an IQ test, the results would come back average at best. I've read about geniuses who earned PhDs before they were twenty-one, young kids who spoke many languages fluently, and whiz kids who could do anything with computers. I always wished I could be like them."

"Well, I have good news for you."

"Don't tell me I could ever be like those people, because that would be unrealistic."

"That's not what I was going to say, George. The good news is that you can increase your IQ. This has been proven."

"Really?"

"That's right. We hear all the time about the benefits of physical exercise, but we don't hear too much about mental exercise. 'Use it or lose it' isn't just applicable to sex. If you want to increase your brainpower, you have to exercise that, too. Now…let's start with music and piano playing, since this is your major interest, and put stuff like math, computers, and learning languages on the back burner for the time being. If you have time for this other stuff after first doing what you should about bettering yourself as a pianist and musician, then you can address those other things at that time. And if you don't have any extra time, that's a good thing, because it means you're using the time you have in a constructive manner. It also means you'll never be bored, and boredom, George, spells TROUBLE.

"I once went on a camping trip when I was a teenager. A girl on the trip actually sang '99 Bottles of Beer' up until the last bottle. This girl *was* verifiably stupid, and the chanting was a manifestation of her boredom and inability to use her mind—and time—in a more constructive and fulfilling manner. You know, if one had a job in which they had to pick up some heavy things and then bring them back to the same place over and over, an intelligent person would go crazy after a while.

"Unless this was for purposes of physical exercise, most intelligent people want to know that their work serves a purpose and accomplishes something. Even cab drivers and janitors who do so-called menial work, know they're getting something accomplished and that their work provides a necessary service.

"My mom used to work for the government, and told me that some of the employees literally walked the halls all day. There are many people who made more money in government benefits for staying home during Covid than they made on their jobs, so they decided to stay home after things opened up again. A gang of hoodlums from Brooklyn who robbed people in Manhattan once bragged, 'Manhattan makes it; Brooklyn takes it.'

"Even though people like this feel they're 'beating the system,' I can't help imagining that deep down, they feel a void in their lives. Looters know that as many times as they rip off the producers of the world, the difference between them and the latter, is that the latter can keep producing; the former can't.

"So, let's get down to some specifics, George. What do you think of jazz pianists?"

"I really admire them. They're able to improvise on the fly, go off on tangents melodically *and* harmonically, and then find their way back home again. That's real mental gymnastics, if you ask me. But I'm not a jazz pianist. I know that improvisation was a huge thing back in the days of Bach, Mozart, and Beethoven, but this is almost a dying art in classical music these days."

"How are you at sight-reading, George?"

"Lousy. I always dismissed that, and rationalized that it wasn't that important. So I made myself a 'final product' kind of guy. I'd slave away at a piece until it was memorized and polished, and consoled myself with the fact that the audience would never know I was a lousy sight-reader. But the older I became, the more it bothered me. There are hundreds of hours of masterpieces in the repertoire, and it would take me many lifetimes to learn and memorize most of it. At least with sight-reading—even if I didn't polish a piece up to performance level—I could enjoy all of this repertoire by reading it as one reads a book."

"And exercising your brain at the same time."

"Right."

"Okay, do you remember when I told you about the *work-around* strategy that I employed with the violinist? You are to designate one hour per day for sight-reading. We'll increase the time later, and even segue into transposing at sight later on, but this is what you must start with. If most of the standard repertoire is too hard to play at sight without stopping, then start with method books, because at least they're graded, and gradually get more and more difficult. Once you start playing, don't stop for any reason, even if you make some mistakes or have to leave out some notes. The important thing is to keep the rhythm going. Sight-reading forces us to process a whole bunch of information at the same time. The more you do it, the better you get at it.

"And by the way, do you know who was probably the greatest sight reader who ever lived? John Ogdon. I've heard about incredible sight readers, but I always thought that being able to sight-read fiendishly difficult and complex pieces at performance tempo was beyond the bounds of what was humanly possible. Ogdon actually sight-read Sorabji's Opus clavicembalisticum, which is one of the hardest pieces to *play*, let alone sight-read. Here was just a case of someone who processed the printed page to his fingers immediately. He was a freak of nature, and was probably unique in history. But he also suffered from severe mental illness, and I'm sure you wouldn't have wanted to trade places with him.

"Next, George, I want you to drastically limit your viewing of the idiot box. Are there some worthwhile programs? Yes. But the overwhelming majority of what's on there is shit…and I'm not even talking about all the time-wasting commercials.

"I've known people who come home and turn on the boob tube as automatically—as if by reflex—as someone goes to the toilet when they wake up in the morning. It's like saying to the box, 'I'm bored; entertain me.'

"Next, read good books, and not just for entertainment. Read books that you can learn something from. Learning something every day is one strong antidote to boredom. And like laugher, it feels so good.

"I think all this is enough for a start. And if you do this, I guarantee that your IQ will be increased. But don't worry about whether or not you could reach the level of someone like Stephen Hawking. He was in a different field, and as I said in reference to John Ogdon, I'm sure you wouldn't have wanted to change places with him. Remember what I told you about striving for a standard, not to equal or better a particular individual."

"Mildred, we were discussing self-esteem, and I'm sure you'd agree that if someone possesses it, there shouldn't be any reason to lie about themselves or their accomplishments. They have enough going for them that they shouldn't have to."

"That's right, George. They shouldn't have to. But they do anyway. Sometimes it becomes a compulsion, and they do it so often that they probably even believe their own bullshit. I once knew a guy who was very short, fat, bald, and unattractive. He happened to covet stunning women. When I asked him if there were any famous women he had in his mind's eye when imagining his 'type,' he said Jaclyn Smith."

"Well, at least you can't fault his taste, Mildred."

"You're right, George. But in as much as Jaclyn Smith is already taken, I don't believe he was what she had in *her* mind's eye when she would imagine *her* ideal man. Anyway, to make up for his less than debonair looks, he felt he had to play the role of the wealthy wheeler-dealer. On dates, he'd suddenly get a call on his cell phone, then make believe he was discussing million-dollar deals with the caller. But there was only so far his ruse could work. Eventually he'd have to bring a woman back to his 'real' residence, rather than the squalid dump his 'parents owned' and that he was 'just staying in until the work on his penthouse was finished.' Eventually, he'd have to pick up his date in his Mercedes, rather than his parents' Volkswagen, because it was finally 'out of the shop.' And eventually, he'd have to show up at one of the superstar restaurants he was always mentioning, dressed in a Brioni suit he claimed he was partial to, rather than dressing like a bum as an indication of 'not wanting to flaunt his wealth' and 'not wanting to act like he was better than the average man.'

"As I'm sure you've already figured out, George, there was only a limited amount of time in which he could pull this off…and like a Ponzi scheme, it all fell apart when push came to shove. But there *are* times when I feel that lying is not only not morally wrong, but actually advantageous. At these times, I would actually recommend it."

"Yes, I know what you're going to say, Mildred. If a criminal breaks into your house and says, 'Where are the diamonds?' there's no obligation to tell the truth. In fact, it'd be stupid to do so."

"You're right, George. To *not* lie in these circumstances would be stupid. But these examples aren't what I'm referring to. Everyone knows we have no obligation to tell the truth to those who want to hurt us, and that we have an obligation to ourselves to say anything we have to say to extricate ourselves from the situation. But let's examine other scenarios that would be appropriate. There are some people, for example, who strongly argue that 'little white lies' shouldn't be told, because it undermines your integrity and just leads to bigger lies.

"One time I was at a party, and a woman begged me to try her chocolate cake. She claimed she made the best chocolate cake anyone had ever made, and that

I was looking at someone who'd probably be famous very soon, as she was about to start selling it to all the top restaurants in the city. Soon she'd have private requests for celebrations, articles would be written about her in newspapers and magazines, and she'd be asked to write a cookbook with her recipes.

"So I tried it, and as I did, she of course leaned into me for what she expected would be my effusive praise. Well, it was so putrid, had I not been right in front of her I would've spit it out. But unfortunately, under the circumstances, I had to swallow it. I'm glad I didn't throw it up. She then said, 'Well? What do you think?' and I said, 'Delicious.'"

"Bad girl, Mildred. You lied."

"You're right, George. I lied. But I never saw this woman again, and felt pressured to give her the praise she almost demanded. What would've been the point in telling her the truth? Now, had I been her baking instructor, that would've been an entirely different story. The same sort of thing comes up with clothing. Someone will say, 'Isn't this outfit I'm wearing beautiful?' They don't want an honest answer. They want you to agree with them. A mother with her month-old infant will say, 'Isn't she the most beautiful baby you've ever seen?' She's actually ugly, but who's going to say that?

"To give you an even better example of how telling the truth can actually be *un*wise, several years ago I was at a party, and it was a similar situation to the one with the woman and her world's-greatest chocolate cake. This guy was bragging to everyone about his daughter. She was a singer with the most incredible voice; she was going to be famous soon; there would be record deals, awards, and on and on. There was a piano there, and he asked his daughter to prove what an amazing talent she had. He goes to the piano to accompany her, his daughter begins to screech off-key, and everyone proceeds to stare at one another with their eyes bulging and in disbelief. We literally didn't know how to react. If we didn't laugh, we could've been accused of not appreciating their comedy routine. If we *did* laugh, there was the possibility that the guy was actually serious.

"By coincidence, one of the guests was actually a *real* singer. He was operatically trained, and also sang on Broadway. In addition, he was an in-demand voice teacher. I guess he felt the demonstration was an affront to his profession and his art, and he proceeded to tell this guy in no uncertain terms the truth about his daughter's vocal prowess. The father then proceeds to unleash an angry diatribe and hurls insult upon insult at the real singer. He got so unhinged, I thought he was actually going to physically assault him. Then he and his daughter stormed out.

"The fact is, George, this man wasn't seeking the truth about his daughter. He was seeking unearned praise. But the real singer could've been more discreet. If he'd been asked for his opinion point-blank from the father, he could've then discreetly pointed out that she needed some improvement, although the father would've probably still flown into a rage. The best thing he could've done under the circumstances was to just mutter, 'She's wonderful' and leave it at that. She wasn't his voice student, he'd never see her again, and he'd never have to worry about her brilliant talent putting him out of business.

"And to give a more personal example, it's of course not morally wrong to lie to a Poker Queen or people of that ilk. In fact, I highly commend Tony for saying whatever he had to say to get you your money back, and I admire his skill and creativity. But I'm not through yet."

"Gee, Mildred, I'm beginning to think you're my lying coach."

Mildred laughed. "It does sound like that, doesn't it? But I do happen to believe in honesty, George. The examples I'm giving you are ones in which our integrity isn't threatened, we don't owe anything to the other party, and we can actually be hurt if we *don't* lie. Consider the following scenario: You're on a date, and you're attracted to the woman. The conversation is flowing. At the end of the date, you say, 'I'd love to see you again.' She then informs you that there's no chemistry. Obviously, to ask why is the *worst* thing a man could do. It doesn't *matter* why, because another woman might love you for the identical reasons this woman doesn't. So to press her on the issue constitutes begging, and this is the last thing you want to do on a date.

"When a woman tells you there's no chemistry, it usually means they're not attracted to you physically. If you're physically attracted to *her*, don't then state you are. You'd now be making yourself seem inferior to her. The best comeback would be, 'I don't feel any chemistry either, but the reason I asked is because I find you very interesting and really enjoyed speaking with you.' This guy gave it right back to her, not giving any more than he got, but in a positive way. And the part about enjoying speaking with her *was* true.

"Now, let's put a little twist on this scenario. A man meets a woman on a date. He's super attracted to her physically. At the end of the date, he says he'd love to see her again. She says, 'I'm sorry. I'm really only interested in dating really good-looking guys in top shape. You don't look at all like your pictures, and in the future, you really shouldn't misrepresent yourself.'

"That's really brutal," said George.

"It is," said Mildred. "And it was uncalled for. Now, assuming she wasn't drop-dead gorgeous, and the guy could pull it off, a good comeback would be, 'I'm not physically attracted to you either. In fact, the other women I've been meeting were all so much better-looking. But I honestly found most of them to be very shallow and self-centered. In addition, most of their 'looks' didn't carry over to their intelligence. The reason I was interested in *you* is because intelligence, and being able to engage in stimulating conversation, is so important to me. But I wish you luck in your search anyway.'

"Now, George, even if the guy *did* consider this woman to be drop-dead gorgeous, and he *was* wildly physically attracted to her, why assuage her ego? He wasn't going to get another date anyway, so why give more than he got, especially since she was cruel and indiscreet? His answer cast doubt in her mind about her *own* looks. If he had merely said, 'Well, you don't look so great either,' she would've just construed this as him trying to save face. But the fact that he threw in the stuff about her intelligence lent authenticity to his comeback. Even though he stuck an insult about her looks into his retort, it made it seem like he was paying her a compliment, because he indicated that intelligence and being able to engage in stimulating discussions was more important to him than looks.

"But my favorite example of lying as a form of self-preservation involved a former patient of mine. It also turned out to be the epitome of 'poetic justice.' When he was in graduate school, he fell hopelessly in love with one of the most stunning women he had ever seen. His very existence was predicated on having her. But sadly, his feelings weren't reciprocated, even though she dangled vestiges of hope.

"To make a long story short, he was in such unbearable pain that suicide seemed like his only alternative. He was literally unable to attend his classes, and had no choice but to come back to New York. He came to see me, and I had to use all my powers of persuasion to convince him that he would eventually get over this. I explained to him that he did not have the benefit of hindsight, but assured him that when he looked back upon this episode years from now, he'd not only be very glad he didn't kill himself, but would reproach himself for being so silly as to allow another person to affect him so much.

"Well, fast-forward twenty-five years later: This formerly overweight and bald guy with a large gap between his two front teeth is now slim and fit, with a full head of transplanted hair, and he also got his gap fixed. In addition, this formerly poor and destitute guy who didn't have a pot to piss in became a successful speaker. One of the places he was booked to speak was at his alma mater. At the end of the speech, a woman comes up to him and calls out his name. 'I'm so and so,' she says. 'Do you remember me?'

"He does remember her name, but wouldn't have ever recognized her now. The stunning woman from twenty-five years ago is now fat, unattractive, and the kind of woman he'd never be interested in dating, much less be in a relationship with. Suddenly, it hit him like a ton of bricks, and he actually discerned the resemblance.

"The woman kept trying to jog his memory, but to no avail. Finally, the guy says, 'Please forgive me. I'm so sorry, but I don't remember you.' She then asks him out for lunch. He thanks her for the offer and for coming to his speech, but says that unfortunately he had to be someplace in a half hour.

"Anyway, when he gets back to New York, he calls and says he has to see me in person. He comes over, throws his arms around me, and gives me such a big hug that I think he's going to crush my bones. I said, 'What happened? Did you win the lottery?' and he answers, 'No, something better.' We literally had a champagne toast.

"George, I once told you that some of the things I've experienced with patients is what I live for. Do you remember what I told you about 'convenient amnesia?' Well, this was a textbook scenario of *deliberate* amnesia.

"By the way, one of the books I told this patient to read when he originally came to me was *The Fountainhead*. Do you remember what Howard Roark says to Ellsworth Toohey when the latter invites him to tell him what he thinks of him in any words he wished?"

"Yes! He says, 'But I don't think of you.' And that is the best thing he could have said."

"And 'not remembering' this woman, George, is the best thing my patient could have done.

"You know, George, we always hear and read about the immorality, so to speak, of lying. On a basic level, and in the manner these people are talking about, they're right. If a man lies about his age in order to date a woman who otherwise would have considered him too old, the deception will eventually come out if this date leads to a relationship or marriage. If a person lies about their educational credentials to land a coveted job, these things can be checked.

"A pathological liar always has to cover their tracks, which often leads to more lies. He or she then becomes a prisoner, so to speak, of the people they're lying to. The person isn't 'good enough' in their own self-evaluation, so they have to pretend to be something they're not in order to garner unearned approval. The problem with this, George, is that this contradicts what self-esteem is all about. Even when a lie or deception is pulled off, and the other party admires you for what they *think* you are, the liar is not let off the hook scot-free. This is because they usually cannot lie to themselves. I use the word *usually*, because there are, as you know, some people who are so good at lying that after a while, they actually convince themselves that their façade is true. O. J. Simpson is a case in point. But with others, as with the 'wheeler-dealer' I told you about, they know full well that they aren't who they portray themselves to be. Even when they pull off their charades for a period of time, they can't escape the condemnation from their most significant critic, namely themselves.

"But if someone might condemn me for advocating lying, they would do well to consider the context. As the examples I relayed to you indicate, not all lying is the same. Look at actors and actresses. Are they not portraying and pretending to be someone they're not? Are they not *technically* lying? Don't the best 'liars' go on to win Academy Awards? Don't aspiring actors go to schools to learn how to become better liars?"

George had remembered the discussions he had had with Mildred, when two years later he met the owners of a restaurant that he used to play the piano at. At this restaurant was a waitress he detested, and who in turn, detested him. All the staff was aware of this, and the owners would always tease him about it. They would say, "George, such and such is 'available,'" and the rest of the staff would laugh.

During this chance encounter, they mentioned that this woman (who had happened to be a good friend of theirs) had died. George looked quizzically at them. The male owner said, "Surely, you must remember her" and tried to describe her to jog his memory.

He shook his head, and said, "Gee, I really don't recall who you're talking about."

The following week, George met Mildred for another session. She offered hot chocolate with whipped cream along with chocolate chip cookies.

"Sorry if this interferes with your diet," she said.

"It does, actually," said George. "But the hot chocolate and cookies are part of my 'Mildred experience,' and any calories gained are totally offset by what I learn from you.

"Mildred, what is your definition of happiness?"

"Ah, the age-old question philosophers have been pondering for centuries. There have been hundreds of books written on the topic, but people still don't know how to define it. And those who try, often come to different conclusions and interpretations. You've really put me on the spot. But since you asked me, and since I'm a philosopher, I feel I should be able to at least attempt an answer.

"The issue of happiness, George, is a tough nut. Knowing what happiness is isn't enough if we don't know how to achieve it. But let's start with the definition. Happiness is a feeling of contentment and peace.

It in no way means that everything in life is a nonstop bed of roses. Happy people experience grief because of the loss of a loved one, the pain of being fired from a job, being injured, and the million and one other things that are a part of life. But the things that happen in life—and boy, do things happen, especially things beyond our control—are not the arbiters of a happy person's mindset; they don't define who they are.

"You've heard me use the term 'irreducible primary' a lot. Well, their general attitude and state of being isn't defined by external things…just like the person of high self-esteem isn't immobilized by whatever a random stranger might say to them. Happiness and self-esteem are intertwined. People who possess this feel worthy of life and up for the challenge. They don't view setbacks and failures as defining elements of who they are as a person. While some people treat defeats as personal failures and reasons to give up their dreams, the happy person with high self-esteem views the same things as challenges to be overcome. And even if they don't always achieve all their goals, their self-esteem indicates that they have the *ability* to achieve them; they believe in their efficacy.

"We've all heard the sayings that money doesn't buy happiness and that the best things in life are free.

You'll find that happy people are able to derive pleasure and be inspired by things that other people aren't. When I was a kid, I once looked at a super-cute baby. She was in a carriage, and her mother was nearby. Well, seeing me, this baby gave me one of the most beautiful, heartfelt smiles anyone's ever given me. I froze the moment in my mind because it was precious. And I've never forgotten the incident.

"I've witnessed full rainbows on mountaintops at dawn. I savored the smell of the air, the miraculous panoramic views, and the feeling of being one with nature. I've made love with Jim in these environments, and at those times I didn't need any philosophers analyzing what the definition of happiness is. I've been moved to tears by the music of great composers. It touched me to the very depths of my soul. At those times, I didn't have to have anyone explain to me the truth of Heinrich Heine's quote, 'Where words leave off, music begins.'

"Once, when I was a teenager, I was driving some friends someplace and put on one of those miraculous pieces on the radio. A girl said to me, 'Could you turn that shit off? I'm getting a headache.' There you have it; two people reacting totally differently to the same thing. Now, that doesn't mean she should love the same things I do; everyone's different. This girl happened to love acid rock and going to concerts where the decibel level could damage your hearing. I myself consider *this* 'music' to be shit. But the point is, it doesn't matter what someone's inspired or passionate about, as long as they *have* something to be inspired and passionate about."

"Mildred, I know what you're saying regarding a person who's basically happy. Their happiness comes from within, as does self-esteem, and isn't affected by external factors. But what about people who are dealt a really bad hand? Seeing family members killed in front of them, going blind, having no arms and legs, things like that? I can imagine a person being truly happy, but can't imagine how someone could be so if they were dealt such a devastating hand. I've always imagined I could be happy if I had things like money, a beautiful home, a loving wife and kids, a great career, and good health. But then I think I might've only been happy because of the circumstances. I wouldn't have been *truly* happy, because I couldn't conceive of being capable of being so if I were dealt a really bad hand.

"For example, I can't imagine being happy if I were blind. When I think about it, I consider it to be one of the worst things that can happen to someone. How would I do my laundry? How would I shop for clothing or food? I'd always be dependent on others to drive me places. I'd never know what anyone looked like. Not being able to experience the joy of seeing a beautiful painting or mountaintop is one thing. But being limited as to getting around, traveling, knowing where I'm going, etc., is beyond what I think I'd be able to tolerate. Yet many blind people have done the most incredible things and are truly happy.

"I'd say the same thing regarding people without arms and legs. How do they go to the bathroom and do basic things? But there are people like that who've similarly achieved great things *and* are happy. Look at Stephen Hawking. He was once asked point-blank, 'Are you happy?' And his answer was, 'Yes.' Here you have an example of someone with a body that didn't work, but with an incredible mind, whose discoveries and knowledge of the cosmos has had, and will continue to have, a profound impact on generations to come."

"You pose very important questions, George, and I've had the same thoughts. I'm a happy person, but would I still be happy if a terrible, life-altering thing happened to me? I'd like to think so, but couldn't guarantee it if I weren't placed in that situation. So I'd be lying if I said I could definitively answer you in the affirmative. You know, sometimes an unspeakable tragedy happens. A woman's daughter is brutally murdered, raped, and dismembered. Sometimes, someone who means well will tell the person, 'I know how you feel.' No, that person does *not* know how it feels. Intellectually, they can understand and imagine the pain this person's going through. But when you're speaking of unbearable, unfathomable pain and suffering, one does not and *cannot* feel this pain unless it happens to you personally.

"And sometimes there are situations when a person is terminally ill. They're suffering, in pain, and there's no reasonable hope the person can get better. Euthanasia, in instances like this, *if* it's something the patient wants, is appropriate. It's a personal decision. It doesn't mean the person is giving up on life and isn't a happy person. It means they don't want to depend on people to take them to the bathroom, feed them, and clean them when there's no possibility of them getting better. If someone is artificially kept alive on a respirator, is it really living because they're *technically* alive?

"But in the case of someone who isn't terminally ill, but suffers a tragedy such as losing their sight or limbs, it's quite understandable for someone to grieve and ask, 'Why me?' But ultimately, there comes a time when you have to accept cold, hard, brutal reality. Do I live or do I die? Do I give in or do I fight to make the best out of my life with what I have? What would I do in a situation like this, George? I'd like to think I'd choose to fight. But like I said in regard to the people who tell others that they know how they feel, you never really know how it feels unless you're personally experiencing it.

"Life isn't fair, George. Sometimes luck and randomness play a role in whether someone becomes successful or not. When Vladimir Horowitz was young, he substituted at the last minute for an indisposed pianist who was scheduled to perform Tchaikovsky's Concerto in B-Flat Minor. He created a sensation, and he's said that if it weren't for this concert, his career might not have amounted to anything. Here you have one of the most legendary pianists in history saying that a random occurrence might've changed the whole trajectory of his life. And then you have people who are less talented in a particular endeavor than someone else. But the former becomes more successful than the latter because of intangibles like 'looks,' personality, and connections. The casting couch is a very real thing in Hollywood, as well as in other professions.

"What I'm trying to say with all of this, George, is that we can't control everything that goes on around us. Random events happen which can permanently alter a life in a heartbeat, positively or negatively. In business, more-deserving people will be passed over for promotions by less-deserving people. Innocent people will be the victims of crimes. Often, criminals will get away with their crimes. People die at different ages. People are shortchanged at birth. The list goes on and on.

"But, with all the things that go on around us that we can't control or directly control, there are still things we *can* control, such as maintaining our self-esteem and integrity in the face of anything that happens, and what our attitude will be in any situation. I've seen motorists cursing, screaming, pounding the steering wheel, and going crazy in traffic jams. Others pop in a CD of a stimulating lecture, or practice learning a foreign language…the same situation, a different attitude and result."

"Mildred, one of the most famous self-help gurus once stated that we're responsible for everything that happens to us."

"Another one of those highly misleading quotes that has elements of truth in it, but is also downright wrong. Yes, the actions we take have a huge impact on whether or not we become successful, or whether or not we achieve a particular goal. So the saying that we create our own luck is largely true, even though there *is* such a thing as bad luck; because the harder we work, and the more positive things we do in pursuit of a goal, the more our 'luck' increases proportionately. So, when we already have the goods, when we work hard, when we do constructive things, then the law of averages *will* tilt in our favor.

"Now, in regard to the statement that we are responsible for everything that happens to us, if someone rides the subway in a deserted train in a slum neighborhood at three o'clock in the morning, or takes a stroll in Morningside Park at the same time, they're greatly increasing their chances of being killed. In such instances, I can conceive of those people being responsible for what happened to them, even though they didn't deserve it, because they engaged in highly dangerous behavior. But if someone's walking down a crowded avenue at noon, someone else can still run out from nowhere and hit them over the head with a baseball bat. I wouldn't consider this victim to be at all responsible for what happened to them, because in no way did they engage in dangerous or risky behavior. Sometimes there's literally no way to anticipate or avoid something like this from happening unless someone never gets out of bed. And even then, a bullet can go through the window and kill them, as happens all the time in this country."

"Mildred…"

"Yes, George?"

"Thank you."

"You're so welcome, honey."

They held each other in a long embrace. Then George walked toward the door. "George?" she called out.

"Yes, Mildred?"

"We're having another concert and party on November 13. We'd like you to play for us."

"Of course, Mildred."

"But this time, Jim and I would like you to include 'Feux follets.'"

"Are you serious?"

"Quite serious, so get to work. This will be ample payment for our sessions."

He walked down the corridor, opened the front door, and felt and breathed in the brisk fall air on Mercer Street. The sudden contrast mirrored his new perspective. Life would still be full of challenges and setbacks, but now he felt ready to face them.

Acknowledgment

I'd like to thank my editor, Jason Pettus, for his expertise and advice. His guidance was invaluable in ensuring that the final manuscript was as good as it could be.